I0587530

FRANKLIN VERSUS THE CHILD THIEF

THE CHRONICLES OF FRANKLIN: BOOK THREE

LEAH R CUTTER

KNOTTED ROAD PRESS

Franklin Versus The Child Thief
The Chronicles of Franklin: Book Three
Copyright © 2018 Leah Cutter
All rights reserved
Published by Knotted Road Press
www.KnottedRoadPress.com

ISBN: 978-1-64470-001-3

Cover Art:
ID 41487519 © Vasilev | Dreamstime.com
ID 94353761 © Vaclav Volrab | Dreamstime.com
ID 30569437 © Camrocker | Dreamstime.com

Cover and interior design copyright © 2018 Knotted Road Press
http://www.KnottedRoadPress.com

Come someplace new...
If you'd like to be notified of new releases, sign up for my newsletter.

I will never spam you or use your email for nefarious purposes. You can also
unsubscribe at any time.

http://www.LeahCutter.com/newsletter/

Seattle Trolls

The Changeling Troll

The Princess Troll

The Fairy-Bridge Troll

The Cassie Stories

Poisoned Pearls

Tainted Waters

Spoiled Harvest

Bloodied Ice

Contemporary Fantasy

Siren's Call

The Immortals' War

Circle of Air

CHAPTER 1

FRANKLIN SAT IN THE BACK, BEHIND HIS HOUSE, watching the night come in. The October sun set earlier every day, tinting the clouds orange that evening. Trucks on the highway passed with a swishing sound, while a few brave crickets still sang of the summer long gone. Mr. Wilkerson, just across the road, already had a fire going, trails of clean burning wood smoke hanging in the air.

The corn in the field in front of Franklin had long since been harvested and dried. It had been a good summer with two full crops. Franklin was still experimenting with the ears, trying to find the perfect combination of timing and heat for making the world's best popping corn.

The white metal chair Franklin sat on grew colder as the chill set in. The world grew quiet and still. Franklin breathed in the peace, wishing he could just bottle it up for those times when he needed it, or to share with his family who sometimes needed it more.

Finally, the boy ghost appeared. He'd been haunting Franklin's place for a few days now.

He was young, stuck in that spot between boy and man, maybe eleven, maybe thirteen. Skinny, white, with a hungry look. The kind who missed his mama but would never admit it. Not 'til he was all growed up, and he weren't gonna have that chance. Not now.

He wore summer clothes still, T-shirt and shorts, his legs all scratched up from running through weeds.

It was just one of the things that worried Franklin about the boy. Ghosts always showed up in what they was buried in.

What family buried a boy in play clothes? All of the other kids who came haunting Franklin wore little suits or pretty dresses.

Not looking as though they'd just run through a field, trying to get away from something.

"It's all right," Franklin told the boy, as he had every night when the boy showed up.

The ghost just shook his head. He stared hard out into the remains of the corn field.

If the boy would just walk forward a few feet, Franklin knew he'd find a better place. The ghost would be able to move on, out of this world and onto the next.

But the boy wouldn't walk forward. And he wouldn't tell Franklin his *intent*.

Usually, the ghosts who came to see Franklin needed a little something to help them move on. That was Franklin's gift—he could hear a ghost's *intent*, silently spoken in his ear. He'd never met a ghost who could say a word out loud or make much noise. They just communicated with Franklin after a fashion, letting him know what they needed before they could go.

Earlier that summer, there'd been an old black man who'd come visiting. Franklin had given the ghost a ride on the back of his bicycle to the barbershop in town, so the ghost could sit there with his friends, listening to their jokes and gossip, one last time. Then there'd been that young white guy, heavy set. Franklin had made him a bowl of popcorn. The ghost had sucked up every last bit of salt and lard, needing one last snack before he could take those final steps.

This boy though, wouldn't state his *intent* or what he needed so he could move on.

Not because he were being stubborn, no, but because he just didn't know.

All Franklin got from the boy was *scared*. He was scared of moving forward. Scared of going back. That fear held him rigid.

"You're gonna be fine," Franklin told the boy.

The ghost shook his head again.

Franklin knew better than to rush a ghost. They was like any growing thing, coming into their time on their own.

So Franklin sat in the growing dark, the stars peeking out, the night closing in around him. The ghost had a soft glow, lighter than most, as if all the boy's life had already been burned out. Which were another thing that bothered Franklin. Child's light should have been brighter than most, not so dim.

What had happened to the boy? How could Franklin do his duty and help this poor child?

After a bit, Franklin stood up. The night brought power to his fields, made the ghosts stronger when they tried pushing their *intent* at Franklin. It weren't as though a ghost could make Franklin do something he didn't want to, but they left him feeling sticky and covered in cobwebs.

While Franklin didn't like being out back after it got dark, he was less spooked than he'd once been. Maybe it was because he'd been seeing more ghosts over the past few years. Maybe it was because after dealing with evil spirits and evil blades, Franklin knew there weren't much out there to be frightened of.

"I'm gonna go back inside," Franklin said out loud. "You take care now."

The ghost stayed standing where he was, staring hard out into the night.

Franklin just shook his head and made his way around the side of the house.

Out of the corner of his eye, Franklin caught a glimpse of Sweet Bess, the huge sow who still haunted his property. Normally, Franklin only saw ghosts of people. Sweet Bess was the one spirit he saw on a regular like basis.

He weren't sure what would get her to move on, if she even wanted to. He called her Sweet Bess because of how sweet her rendered fat had turned out. When she'd been alive, she'd been anything but sweet, killing pretty much every small animal who came across her path, and some big ones as well.

It was strange, but Franklin had the feeling that she acted as a guard dog sometimes. Like tonight. She circled the house as if guarding it. From what, Franklin didn't have a clue. Or even if there was something out there, some spirit that he needed protecting from.

Mind you, the huge sow still occasionally decided that she didn't want Franklin going into his own damned house.

Franklin had the impression that when Sweet Bess turned on him, as she had just last month, it was as much for fun as anything else. She'd wanted to play, to run at him and make him turn tail and haul ass out of there because it made her laugh in her own piggy way, not because she was angry at him for butchering her.

Not any more mad than usual.

Tonight, Bess was just making her rounds. If he bothered to watch, she'd pace around the house through the rest of the night, not disappearing until the sun came back up.

Franklin almost felt sorry for any spirit who tried to get through her.

The main door to the house led straight into the kitchen. The front door, located in the living room, was barely used. There was even a big overstuffed chair in front of it, as there had been for most of Franklin's life.

The light above the stove was still on. After Mama had died, she'd spent all her time as a ghost sitting at the kitchen table, providing her own soft glow. Now that she'd truly moved on, Franklin kept the light on in the kitchen to give him some comfort.

Though he didn't need that reminder of comfort and home as much. Not anymore.

Franklin no longer lived here alone. He shared the house with Julie, his wife. They'd been married for more than two years, after dating for another two.

He was thankful for her every single day.

She was working a late shift at the hospital tonight. She still worked as an ER nurse, still an adrenaline junkie, even after she'd gotten pregnant. Though now her thrills included taking a Saturday off to cuddle on the couch with her husband.

And the things they'd do afterward, which still made Franklin blush just to think about.

Good thing his black skin hid most of that.

The kitchen had dishes regularly in the drying rack. Not just a single plate or pan, but two or four plates and glasses and forks. The smell of weekly pot roast made the place seem more homey. Two bright red towels hung from the handle of the stove—they was a lot nicer than what Franklin had had, and colorful, too.

If Franklin had to sum up what Julie brought to his life in a single word (other than love) he'd have to say "color." She made his life brighter.

Moving from the kitchen, Franklin walked through the dining room. A long table was pushed to the side, under the windows, the chairs trapped in place. It used to be covered with an old, yellowing, plastic tablecloth that was easy to wipe clean. Now, the table was uncovered, ready to be used. He and Julie had been hosting the family Sunday dinners about once a month.

Aunt Jasmine had been hesitant about letting them at first. She later admitted it weren't because she didn't like Julie, even though she was a white girl. It was because Aunt Jasmine just weren't sure if Julie could learn to cook things proper.

Fortunately, Julie had been happy to learn, and could now make a mean casserole. Her roasts were liked by everyone, even the kids.

Though Franklin would never say so out loud, Julie's biscuits were now turning out just a shade better than his aunt's. Almost as good as Mama's. He could think of no higher praise.

The old couch in the living room had been replaced with a new loveseat, fit for just the two of them. (And the memory of Julie insisting that they break it in proper still made Franklin warm.) The TV was new too, a flat screen that hung on the wall, the bureau the old set had sat on long gone.

Julie had never insisted that Franklin make those changes. He'd just started, all on his own, making space in his house, in his life, for her.

And now, they were making space for the young one who would be joining them soon.

A baby rocker sat in the corner. There was the smell of new

plastic from the collection of toys that Julie's co-workers had given her at the baby shower.

Franklin had had no idea that a baby needed so much stuff.

Before Julie had finally moved in with Franklin, he'd rearranged the bedrooms for the pair of them.

All his life, Franklin had lived in the smaller bedroom. It hadn't seemed respectful taking the bigger one, particularly not when Mama had still been haunting him.

Just before Julie moved in, Franklin switched rooms. Bought them a brand new queen-sized bed too, because while the king sized might have been nice, he wanted to sleep closer to his wife. Julie had brought most of the bedroom furniture from her place, a pretty white set that all matched.

Franklin had never had a matching set of anything before. Except socks. Maybe.

Instead of going into his—their—bedroom and getting in a nap before Julie came home, Franklin went to what had once been his old room. He turned on the light and just stood in the doorway, marveling at how different it all looked.

A crib stood to his right, along with a table for changing diapers. Aunt Jasmine, his cousins, and the people from church had all contributed something for this room, clothes and such. The toys weren't brand new, so instead of smelling like plastic, they smelled like baby powder. The mobile above the crib came from Julie's dad who was a mechanic. He'd carved all the pieces himself out of light wood, each one a different vintage car, brightly painted.

High in the corner of the room, almost opposite the door, was a smudge stick, about six inches long, made out of white sage leaves tied tightly together. Julie's other friends, Eddie and the rest of the pagan group, had come up one Saturday and blessed the entire house.

While Franklin didn't believe in all their gods (and maybe he were still a touch angry at Eddie for putting Julie into danger by just handing her that evil knife and not warning her) he knew the group's *intent* was right, that they didn't mean no harm and just wanted to help.

Thin branches of rowan wood braided together sat on the windowsills. They was supposed to keep the spirits away. Franklin suspected they was useless: no mere wood was ever gonna keep out a determined spirit.

Then again, when ghosts did visit the inside of the house, they never went into this room. Even after Franklin had moved into the other bedroom with Julie.

Julie and Franklin had torn up the old carpet most everywhere and replaced it with new. The baby room had a soft gray carpet now, one that wouldn't stain. Then they'd painted the walls a soft blue-tinted white, and had one of Julie's co-workers come by and paint stencils of balloons floating across them.

It was a happy room.

Had the boy outside had such a warm place, once? Franklin would bet he had. He didn't have the feral look Franklin saw in the homeless kids who passed through Katherinesville. That boy had been raised in a good home with a loving family.

Franklin couldn't shake the feeling that something bad had happened to the boy. He didn't have the look of a child long sick. He still had all his hair, for one. And then there were his clothes.

All through the summer and now into the fall, Franklin had been seeing a lot more ghosts who were children. It was doubly —tripley—some number Franklin knew but couldn't count to —difficult, seeing young ghosts, particularly since he had his own child on the way.

Had the younger ghosts started showing up because there would be a baby in the house soon? Did like attract like? Or was there something else going on, something that Franklin didn't even want to think about?

Franklin nearly jumped out of his skin when a trilling noise sounded behind him. It took a couple of rings before Franklin finally managed to answer his damned cell phone.

That was one of the changes he'd made for Julie at her request—getting one of them new-fangled smart phones, the kind Mama always said made you stupid.

Franklin didn't use it much, well, except to text Julie. And to listen to Aunt Jasmine when she needed to bend his ear about something. Or when Darryl called with some wild hair of an idea.

Like now.

Franklin grinned as he answered. "So what's up, Darryl?" He was proud of the fact that he always knew who was calling him now. 'Cause if he didn't recognize the number, he didn't bother answering. Seemed that it was always someone trying to sell him something he didn't need.

"Franklin?" Darryl's voice came across the line, high pitched.

Scared.

Franklin took a deep breath. "Yeah, it's me," he said. He settled in, took a wider stance, braced himself. "What happened?"

It couldn't be Aunt Jasmine, could it? After Mama died of a heart attack at such a young age, her older sister had started taking care of herself. She'd lost weight and begun going to jazzercise with "all them skinny white bitches" according to her.

"Tommy's missing," Darryl said. "We can't find him. *I* can't find him."

Franklin swallowed against a throat suddenly gone dry.

Too many children gone missing lately.

"When was the last time you seen him?" Franklin asked as he started making his way back toward the kitchen. He didn't like riding his bike so late at night, but his cousin needed him there. Even if there weren't nothing Franklin could do.

"We sent him and Pete to bed early for acting up," Darryl admitted. "Just went to check in on them. Pete's still there, snoring. Tommy ain't. Oh god," Darryl said, his voice breaking. "Can't be that the last thing I said to my oldest boy was that I was mad at him."

"You tried hunting for him?" Franklin asked.

"I said I had, didn't I?" Darryl said. He sounded mad, now. "I can track damned near anything. But I can't find my boy."

"I'm on my way," Franklin assured Darryl as he stepped out of the house.

Julie would understand. Hell, she'd probably beat him over to Darryl's place.

Lights suddenly shone in the driveway. Darryl's black truck came barreling in.

"No need, Cuz," Darryl called through the open window.

Franklin nodded and made his way over to the truck.

When Franklin's cousin Lexine had died, she'd had a will and left a pile of money. Then, Aunt Jasmine had sold the place. Darryl had bought a new truck. Aunt Jasmine had paid off most of her house, then given some to the church and the rest to her kids.

Though the truck was only a couple of years old, it looked beat to hell. Darryl liked hunting and weren't particular about the back roads he drove on. Probably barreled through, making his own on occasion.

"Why'd you come to get me?" Franklin asked as he climbed in. "I could've ridden over."

"I know," Darryl said. "I thought maybe, if I was driving around, I could catch a scent or something."

Franklin shook his head. "That ain't smart and you know it, Cuz," he said. "Besides, I don't want you catching a trail and driving this thing over the neighbors' yards. Again."

Darryl threw Franklin a grin as he pulled out of the gravel driveway with enough speed to make the tires spin. "That's why you're here. To make sure I don't do anything crazy."

Franklin stared at Darryl in amazement. "You know that if anyone heard you say that, they'd think you was nuts, right? Making me the sane one here?"

Franklin's family knew that there was something special about Franklin, just as there had been something special about Lexine. A lot of the town knew as well, since Mama would brag on her boy when she'd been alive and working at the hair salon. She were proud of him though, doing his duty with the ghosts.

However, the ghosts was also the main reason why Franklin didn't have a car. He knew how to drive, kept his license regularly renewed. However, it was a lot easier to fall off a bicycle if he got startled by a ghost rather than running off the road into traffic and maybe hurting someone.

"I just...I needed someone with me. When we get back," Darryl said.

Franklin reached over and wrapped his hand around Darryl's bicep, squeezing lightly. "We'll find him."

Darryl nodded, his look turning grim.

Or at least, Franklin hoped they'd find Tommy. On this side of the grave.

CHAPTER 2

FRANKLIN TEXTED JULIE ABOUT TOMMY BEING MISSING and that he'd gone to help the search. She let him know that she'd be there as soon as her shift was over, though she'd been asked to stay late. Again.

Darryl pulled up into his driveway. The bikes for the two boys was leaning up against the garage door. Georgia, Darryl's wife, had her car parked there, too. The cars rarely made it into the garage—that was Darryl's "man cave," where he kept all his tools. He'd gotten rid of most of his guns awhile ago, switching over to hunting with a bow and arrow. He could track a critter, any critter, with a speed and grace that no mere ordinary person could match.

And Darryl practiced at it. That much Franklin knew. There was a long story that Darryl had told Franklin once, and even then, only after too much beer, about the deer he'd let get away. Usually, Darryl caught whatever he'd set his mind to catching. But this deer, she'd been special, and Darryl had felt he'd passed some sort of "spirit test" by letting her go.

That Darryl couldn't find Tommy meant they needed to

search harder, or wider, or something. Darryl should have gotten a good hold of the boy's trail.

All the lights in the rambler were on. Some of the other houses on the street were already dark, neighbors who had a long commute in the morning long since gone to bed. Aunt Jasmine's old green Ford wasn't there, so Franklin assumed that Georgia hadn't called her yet.

"Have you found him?" Darryl asked as soon as they walked in the door.

"No."

Georgia sat on the couch with her arms wrapped around herself. She was a solid black woman who wouldn't take any lip from any of her boys, Darryl included. She looked older that night, with her hair unpinned, her work skirt and blouse still on.

Franklin wondered if losing a child would age them all ten years or more overnight.

Pete lay on the couch next to his mother, sound asleep, curled up around a blanket that had probably been covering him earlier. He looked so much younger than nine years old, his black face slack, his skin fresh.

Georgia pushed herself up from the couch to go to Darryl. "I've called all Tommy's friends, seeing if he'd gone over there. But no one has seen him. I've checked the backyard. The garage. Everywhere." She sighed. "I even woke up Pete to see if he knew anything. He's just now gone back to sleep. Joanne went right back to sleep after I checked her room, so I didn't have to bring her out here."

"We'll find him," Darryl said as he wrapped his arms around his wife. They stood there, solid, drawing comfort from each other.

Franklin turned his head to give them a moment together.

He was glad they had each other. And the rest of the family, too.

"You got any ideas?" Georgia said, turning toward Franklin. She always suspected him of instigating at least half of the crazy things that her husband got involved with. Which weren't fair, as Franklin rarely was the one who came up with those ideas in the first place.

"Let's try looking outside for the boy again," Franklin suggested. He didn't want to call it hunting, not in front of Georgia. He didn't know how much Darryl had told his wife about his own abilities.

Darryl nodded and turned, going straight for the door. Franklin followed after him.

He weren't sure if his own abilities would help make Darryl's stronger. They didn't seem to work that way.

He sure as hell hoped he wouldn't see any ghosts around here.

Darryl led the way to the side of the house, then squatted down outside the bedroom window. Tommy and Pete shared a room, while Joanne got one all to herself.

"Shine a light down here, would ya?" Darryl asked.

"I didn't bring a flashlight," Franklin said, turning to go back into the house to fetch one.

"No, you idiot," Darryl said. "You've got one on that phone of yours."

"Oh! Right," Franklin said, pulling it out of his pocket. He still weren't used to it. He typed in the word "loveher" to unlock it, since that password always made him smile.

Before he could figure out how to turn on the flashlight, Darryl had snatched the phone from his hands.

"Here," Darryl said, jabbing something, then handing the phone back to Franklin. "Shine it over my shoulder."

Franklin nodded. He weren't offended by Darryl. He could see that his cousin was frantic with worry.

It was funny. The more worried Franklin got, it seemed like the more calm he got. Deliberate.

Stubborn.

Had Tommy gone through the window? The screen seemed intact. Still, Darryl found something, some clue.

"See this?" Darryl said, pointing to a bit of dirt. Franklin didn't see nothing, but he figured Darryl did.

"He went this way," Darryl said, turning and racing across the yard. He moved with a grace and speed that no one else could match, part of his gift when he was actually on the trail of something.

A tall fence blocked off the house from the neighbors'. Scraggly bushes grew up along the edges, doing their best to cover it. Darryl went directly to the far corner. "Over here," he said.

Franklin followed, using the flashlight to light his own way.

"He went over the fence," Darryl said. He grabbed the top of the fence and pulled himself up, looking out.

"No, he didn't. Trail just ends here," Darryl said looking around. He sounded defeated. "He didn't go over. Just pulled himself up."

"Was he alone?" Franklin had to ask.

Darryl glanced over his shoulder. The darkness hid his hard expression.

Franklin stood still. He knew it was the right thing to ask, just as much as he knew that Darryl hadn't wanted to think about it.

"Yeah, I think so," Darryl said after a moment. "Nobody snatched him."

Franklin shone the light all along the top of the fence.

"What's that?" he asked, shining the light to Darryl's left. Something was sticking out between two of the wooden slats of the fence. It couldn't be seen from anywhere but right up here.

Darryl snaked his hand behind the bush and pulled out a dark square box before he jumped down.

He brought it over to Franklin so they could look at it in the light.

It was a deck of playing cards. A bicycle deck, blue and white, the corners smudged and dirty with use. The cards had been broken in and were not longer stiff, as if someone had shuffled them over and over again.

For a moment, Franklin thought they might have looked familiar. Where had he seen a deck like this before?

"Think these are Tommy's?" Franklin asked Darryl.

Darryl nodded. "Yes," he said firmly.

Franklin believed him. It was one of those things about Darryl, drawing things together, like his hunting.

"What was Tommy doing with a deck of cards? He's not old enough to have a regular poker group, is he?" What Franklin didn't know about kids these days scared him sometimes.

Darryl just shook his head, confused. "We don't play cards," he said slowly. "Poker or anything else. But not because it's forbidden or something." While some folks around these parts held that playing cards was evil, all gambling being the devil's work, Franklin and his cousins hadn't been raised in that kind of church.

Franklin reached out and ran a finger against the top of the deck. There was something there, something special about these cards. They weren't magic. They didn't have a spirit inside them. But there was still something about them, something different.

"How come you didn't see that trail the first time you came out here?" Franklin asked. They could solve the mystery of the cards later. Darryl searching and not being able to find his boy, when he found the trail so easy the second time, was a bigger mystery.

Darryl looked at the cards, looked at the fence, then swung his head back and forth, as if following the trail.

"Goddamn it!" Darryl said, racing back toward the house, heading for the front door. "Because it weren't a trail leading from the house, but one going back in."

Fear raced along Franklin's spine, giving him a chill. He glanced behind him, but he didn't see no ghost standing there breathing down his back.

Darryl ran in the front door hollering. "Tommy! Tommy!"

Franklin came in hot on his heels, following his cousin to the boys' room.

Tommy sat up in the middle of his bed. He gave a long, wide-mouthed yawn. "What's going on?" he asked, all innocent, like he'd just woken up.

Franklin had to give the boy credit. He almost pulled it off. But his eyes were too bright and wide open. Franklin had seen that boy when he'd just woken up. He weren't nearly that awake, generally.

Darryl didn't waste any time, just threw himself on the bed, wrapping his arms around his boy. "You're here," he said.

Franklin felt his own eyes starting to tear up at the emotion in his cousin's voice.

Georgia and Pete brushed past Franklin, the pair of them going directly to the bed, all of them wrapping their arms around Tommy and holding on for dear life.

Franklin's phone rang. It was Julie. He stepped out of the bedroom and into the hallway, giving Darryl and his family time to hold on.

"I'm on my way," Julie told him. He heard the car rev in the background.

"We found Tommy," Franklin told her. "So don't you go setting new speed records getting here."

Julie's dad had zooped up her car a treat. Franklin was always worried that she'd have a blowout one of these days or maybe not be able to talk her way out of a speeding ticket.

"Too late," Julie said. He could hear the laughter in her voice.

Franklin understood what that meant. He walked to the front door and went to stand at the end of the driveway. "How long?" he asked.

"Soon. Bye," Julie said.

He shook his head and then spent at least five minutes figuring out how to turn the damned flashlight off on his phone.

Darryl showed up in the doorway about then. "Thanks," he called out to Franklin. "You need a ride home?"

"Julie's on her way," Franklin told him.

"She setting a new record?" Darryl asked with a grin.

"Probably," Franklin said. For normal people, the hospital was a thirty-minute drive away from Darryl's house.

Julie could do it in under fifteen. Was bucking for ten.

"She should start driving an ambulance," Darryl said.

"Don't you dare suggest that to her," Franklin warned Darryl. His cousin just gave him a bright grin. "I'm serious." He'd worry less with her working in a hospital than driving for a living.

Darryl held up his hands to indicate his surrender. "I won't. I know better than to cross you in a mood like this."

"So what happened?" Franklin asked, walking closer to the door. He didn't think anyone else in the neighborhood needed to hear them talking about Darryl's missing boy. This was a family matter. No concern of theirs.

Darryl sighed deeply and shook his head. "Said he just went out into the yard for a bit. Wouldn't admit to those cards being his, though I know they are. Tommy keeps saying he don't understand what all the fuss is about."

"Is there something going on with your boy?" Franklin asked. The whole family worked hard to keep the kids out of trouble, just as Mama and Aunt Jasmine had done with them. Franklin had resented Mama and her interfering ways when he'd been younger, but he'd never rebelled that much. Not near as much as Darryl and May had.

Besides, Franklin had always had his duty to the ghosts to keep him honest, too.

"I don't know," Darryl said. "I don't think he's doing drugs. He's not in a gang. He gets good enough grades at school. I just don't know what's up with him."

"Want me to try to talk with him?" Franklin offered.

Darryl shook his head. "Naw."

"He might talk with me before he'd talk with his pa," Franklin pointed out.

Darryl pressed his lips together for a moment, as if holding back his denial and his hurt, but he knew Franklin was right.

"We're having Sunday dinner here tomorrow, instead of going to Grandma's," Darryl said.

"Grandma" was always going to be Aunt Jasmine to Franklin, though he knew that Darryl and Georgia had started calling her grandma because of the kids.

Would he, too, start calling her something different once his own baby arrived?

He just didn't know.

"We'll be here," Franklin said as he saw the headlights of Julie's car starting down the street.

His heart was still beating hard as she pulled up. Not because of her, or not just because of her, but because all his worry hadn't yet died down.

What would he do if his own child went missing?

Franklin didn't like even contemplating the consequences he'd be willing to suffer for a child of his own.

CHAPTER 3

Julie yawned and stretched herself before curling back up around Franklin, her head on his shoulder. Her belly pushed out into his side, soft and warm, but still firm. Like it weren't gonna take no guff from him or nobody.

"I don't want to get up," Julie said with a huge yawn.

"Then you shouldn't," Franklin said. He ran his fingers through her soft brown hair, tenderly smoothing it out.

"Yeah, but you should," Julie said, pushing herself up to half sitting.

"How 'bout this?" Franklin asked, pulling Julie back down on top of him. She came easily, still yawning. "Why don't you just sleep in for the rest of the morning? Come meet us at lunch?"

Julie nodded. "I don't mind going with you to church," she said, one hand caressing his bare chest. "It's just that I'm so tired. All the time."

"I understand," Franklin said, letting everything be. Julie actually didn't like going to his church with all the talk of god.

But he didn't like going to her pagan group with all their talk of the many gods.

They compromised, with Julie missing his church and him missing her meetings just as often.

"Sleep," Franklin said, kissing Julie's forehead. "I'll let you know when we get to Darryl's."

Julie nodded and slid her head from Franklin's shoulder to her pillow. "Thank you," she said softly, her eyes already closed.

Franklin pushed himself up to kiss her temple, then made himself get out of bed before he'd be too tempted to stay there with her.

While Julie needed her sleep, his family also needed him, particularly after the worry of the night before with Tommy going missing.

Where had the boy gone? Why hadn't Darryl been able to find him? And what was with that deck of cards? Franklin knew there was something going on.

Franklin took a shower and dressed quietly. Julie wasn't snoring, not exactly. More like a quiet purr. She looked so fresh and young curled up on the bed. Even with the covers pulled up he could still see her big belly.

Child was due in a little less than a month. Unless it was late, which Julie had already warned him might happen. That was frequently the case with new mothers.

Franklin had learned a lot more about pregnant women than he'd ever wanted to, that was for sure.

But he wouldn't have traded his life with anyone else. Not ever.

He threw a kiss at Julie before he left the bedroom, hoping that she felt his love even in her sleep.

For breakfast, Franklin fried up an egg sandwich, with two pieces of toast covered in real butter and cheese with the eggs in between. He brought up the farm report on his phone. He missed listening to it in the morning, the TV a quiet hum in the background, but he didn't want to take the chance on waking Julie up.

Though she looked good, she was tired all the time now. Seemed like most all she did was work and sleep. Then again, she was doing a fine job of growing their baby.

Maybe he should think of it like she had three jobs right now—being a nurse, being a wife, and being a mother—and that she needed her sleep. And then some.

Franklin had dressed in his church clothes, a nice gray suit with a white shirt, no tie, black socks and good loafers that Julie had bought for him. He got his bicycle out of the new storage shack in the front of the house, next to the driveway.

After Ray's wife Adrianna died, Ray had packed up and left town. Ray had left a bunch of boxes that he'd asked Franklin store for him. They held a lot of Adrianna's things, her art and such, that Ray just couldn't face yet.

So Ray bought Franklin a new shack, made from one of those kits that two workers had assembled in a couple of hours. Franklin had tried to give Ray money, but Ray said he would count the storage as payment instead.

The new shack was a pretty blue with white trim. Julie had been trying to grow flowers on the northern side of it, as it was mostly shaded and wouldn't get too warm, even in summer.

Maybe next year they'd take root.

Though the door to the shack had been firmly locked, and the overhead light came on solid and strong, not flickering or nothing, Franklin still took the time to check not only the brakes and wheels of his bicycle, but the chain, too.

He'd never had a ghost who'd been vengeful enough to

harm his bicycle, but he still checked it. Every time. Even if he were late for work. Or church.

Before he left, Franklin went searching through one of his boxes, looking for something of Mama's. He found it, and put it in his pocket for later.

Franklin pushed the bicycle up the gravel driveway and out onto the lane. No cars passed him here. The sky was a pale blue that morning, no hint of fall rains yet, though he knew they were coming back, maybe later in the week. He waved at Mrs. Wilkerson out weeding her yard, then drove out to Stevens, the busier street. He stayed on the far side of the shoulder, as careful now as he'd always been.

It was actually safer once he got to the main highway, as there was a proper bike lane now. He considered waving as he passed by Metzger's Fruit and Vegetable Stand, but no one was there, so he didn't.

Franklin and Karl had talked about renaming the stand since they was equal partners now. Karl had even joked about naming it "Karl and Franklin's Popcorn Emporium."

But Franklin didn't like to make a fuss. He didn't see the need for his name to be up there on the marquee. He and Karl both owned the place, both worked there everyday but Sunday. Franklin just liked the feeling he got when he rode by, knowing it was half his. Part of his living came from plants that he grew, as well as crops from suppliers.

It was how he'd always dreamed he'd make a living. Though he worked a lot of hours, he felt rich because he almost always was doing what he loved.

The church Franklin's family went to was a newer one. That had always made Franklin more easy, as there weren't as many ghosts hanging around. The building was built out of white stone with a tall, arched roof. Plain glass filled most of the windows, the fundraiser to replace them with stained glass continually ongoing.

Aunt Jasmine had spent some of the money from Lexine's property to buy one of the windows, putting it in the family name.

While Franklin was proud of that, he knew Lexine would have just rolled her eyes at having something in her name at the church. She'd been part of the pagan group, with Julie and the others.

Miss Karen and Miss Kay stood outside as always, greeting everyone who came in. They were spinster aunts who Franklin had thought ancient when he'd been a boy. They still looked ageless, with more laugh wrinkles than frown wrinkles, white hair shining like halos and smooth dark skin. They wore proper hats and gloves, neat dresses and sensible shoes. Today, Miss Karen was in all pink while Miss Kay was in purple.

"Morning ladies," Franklin said, coming up after he'd locked his bike up.

"Morning Franklin," Miss Karen said. "How's that young bride of yours?"

"More beautiful every day, ma'am," Franklin said honestly. And she was.

"You let us know after the babe's come. We'll help babysit," Miss Kay offered.

"Thank you, ma'am," Franklin said. "We sure appreciate it."

He didn't think he'd be calling on them anytime soon. It was a nice gesture, that was all.

"We'd be delighted," Miss Karen said, determined to get the last word in.

"We sure would be," Miss Kay called after him.

Franklin was glad his back was turned to them so they

couldn't see his grin at their efforts to be the one who got in the last word.

The Smiths were just inside the door, handing out the programs to everyone coming in. Before Franklin could get out of the cool nave and into the sanctuary, Preacher Sinclair came up.

The preacher wore his purple robes that morning, as well as a white scarf embroidered with golden crosses that hung down to the floor in the front. He had a broad smile and an easy manner, kind of like a used-car salesman, though a touch more sincere.

"Franklin! Good to see you, son," Preacher Sinclair said, tugging Franklin to the side before he could step into the sanctuary.

"Reverend," Franklin said, nodding his head. He found himself widening his stance, preparing himself for a blow, though he knew that Preacher Sinclair wouldn't strike him.

"Can I speak with you? After the service?" the preacher asked.

Franklin didn't like the look in the preacher's eye, as if Franklin were the winning number on the bingo chart.

"Of course, reverend," Franklin said. "I am at your service."

"Thank you," Preacher Sinclair said, walking away.

Damn it! What did the preacher want? Franklin just knew that it wouldn't be good.

With a sigh, Franklin turned back and entered the sanctuary. Light-colored wooden beams lifted the peaked roof, bringing it closer to heaven. The church felt open to him, with not only the aisle in the center but two more, one running down either side of the pews. Windows ran along both sides, bringing in more light. Soothing organ music filled the sanctuary. It smelled of the coffee and donuts being served downstairs. Franklin's stomach reminded him that though he'd eaten breakfast, a little snack wouldn't be amiss.

About midway up the aisle, Franklin spotted his cousin May with her two girls, Carlie and June, her boy Austin, along with her husband Henry. Aunt Jasmine sat at the end of the aisle, the proud matriarch.

After kissing Aunt Jasmine's cheek, Franklin sat in the pew behind May's family. May was still talking with the Jacksons who sat in front of them. He shook hands with Henry and Austin, then said hello the to the girls, who barely paid him no mind. He didn't take offense. They were almost teenagers and none of the adults were cool enough to matter anymore.

They'd learn, as teenagers always did, that the whole world weren't supposed to revolve around them, no matter how much they thought it should.

May wore a halter top dress with a little white cardigan to keep her shoulders warm. While the colors were pretty—lavender and yellow—the dress itself was too tight, too short, and not appropriate for church.

At least her girls were dressed nicely. Franklin wondered how long that would last.

Henry wore a suit like Franklin, though his was older and no longer fit him around the waist. He'd be having to get a new one, in a bigger size, soon. While Austin still wore a nice shirt and slacks.

As soon as May could turn around, she did. "What happened with Tommy last night?" she asked quietly. Normally, May was always teasing Franklin about this, that, or the other. She sounded worried, though.

"Don't rightly know," Franklin said honestly. "He slipped out of the house for a while. Don't know why. Then slipped back in again."

"Was he out smoking?" she said.

"Didn't smell it on him," Franklin said. He knew that May was worried that her oldest, Carlie, had started smoking. No one in the family really smoked—both Mama and Aunt Jasmine had considered it a waste of money and they'd ruled the family with fists of iron. Everyone else had bent to their will.

"Maybe he has a girlfriend," May said after a bit. "Cute boy like that."

"Ewww," Carlie announced. "Who would want to date him?"

"So you don't think he has a girl?" Franklin asked Carlie.

She shook her head. "Nope. I know he's got one he's got his eye on, but she won't give him any sugar."

"I see," Franklin said. Or at least he hoped he did. He was gonna have to learn a whole new vocabulary.

That was all right. His own child would just have to be patient with him.

Franklin's cousin Jason arrived next. It made Franklin's heart glad to see that Elsie, his wife, had come to church as well. She'd gone through a bad spell being sick the last few years. Jason had finally admitted that his wife had cancer. Julie had gone to sit with her, to help her through the chemo. She was the only one Elsie would talk with, maybe because Julie was married into the family, like Elsie.

Elsie was cancer free now, and finally getting back to healthy.

Their two girls were growing up so fast. They looked cute in their yellow and black dresses, their hair done in loose braids. Uncle Franklin was no longer their favorite, a change that had taken place that summer. He didn't know if that were a permanent like thing or just temporary.

Darryl and his family didn't come in until just before the

service started. Franklin didn't think they'd done that on purpose, just so they didn't have to talk with anyone else. They was having Sunday dinner, the location moving from Aunt Jasmine's at the last minute. He supposed they just needed time to prepare this morning.

As usual, Franklin spent the entire sermon arguing in his head with the preacher. Today, the message was all about the importance of faith. Preacher Sinclair started with the lessons of Lot, whose faith wasn't strong enough, so he turned around and his wife turned to salt.

It weren't that the preacher was wrong about the importance of faith. That was what Franklin always was telling his ghosts. They had to believe they was going someplace better and step forward, move into the next plane.

But it wasn't just that they had faith in God. They also had to have faith in themselves. They had to remember that they'd been good people, that they wouldn't end up going to Hell.

Or at least Franklin always believed that the ghosts who came to see him weren't on their way to Hell. They were never scared. Not like that.

Except for that boy. Franklin had never seen a ghost as scared, except for Gloria—three, maybe four years back now —standing in Karl's field, staring at the nest of that evil creature.

What monster had that boy faced? Or who was he afraid to face, which was why he couldn't keep going?

Finally, the sermon was over. Franklin joined the rest of his family in the greeting line.

"You doing okay?" Franklin asked Darryl, sliding over to stand next to his cousin.

"Yeah," Darryl said. He seemed more tired than angry, but Franklin could see the fury still lay there under the surface.

"Tommy won't tell me anything. Won't tell us where he went or why he went out."

"I'll talk with him," Franklin promised. "But, uhm, I gotta talk with the preacher first."

"You doing okay?" Darryl asked. "How's Julie?"

"Tired," Franklin said.

Darryl gave him a grin. "Been through that. Three times. It'll be rough at the start, but you've got family to help."

"Thanks," Franklin said. He knew that Darryl meant it. May, too, would help. And Jason. And Aunt Jasmine. As well as Julie's family, though they lived over an hour away, in the next county.

"Need a ride?" May asked as they finished going through the greeting line.

"Preacher asked to have a word with me," Franklin told her. Though he knew that May's family would make room for him, it would be awfully crowded in their car and Franklin wouldn't feel like he could breathe the whole trip. It would be better to drive to Darryl's on his own, even if it meant riding his bike.

"You not having trouble like you did a couple years ago, are you?" May asked.

"No, ma'am," Franklin said. "I hope not." He weren't about to bring up the child ghost right now haunting him, not until he knew for sure that it was a problem.

Then again, he weren't the type to go asking for help, even when he needed it.

Finally, the last of the congregation made their way along and Preacher Sinclair strode back to the church. "Thank you, Franklin, for waiting for me." He pulled out a handkerchief and mopped his brow. "Let's step inside."

"Sure thing," Franklin said, following the preacher back into the dim church.

They stood in the nave, the only light coming through the open door. Franklin shivered in the cool hall, blinking after the brightness of the sunny day.

"What can I do for you, reverend?" Franklin asked. He didn't want to keep his family waiting. Julie was already on her way to Darryl's house.

"Franklin, have you seen the Chambers' oldest boy?" Preacher Sinclair asked.

"Who?" Franklin said, not sure of who the preacher was talking about.

"Hollis Chambers," the preacher said. "He's a boy, just turned twelve."

"I don't think I know the Chambers," Franklin said. He tried to think if he'd ever met them at church, or maybe at the vegetable stand.

The preacher looked over his shoulder, making sure they were alone in the nave. His tone dropped down even further. "Hollis has been missing for a week now. White boy. Nice blue eyes. Skinny. You seen any ghosts matching that description?"

Franklin blinked, surprised. He wasn't sure that the preacher even believed that Franklin could talk with ghosts. But this weren't the only time that the preacher had asked Franklin if he'd met the ghost of someone who'd recently passed.

Generally, the people in the congregation who passed was already at peace. They didn't have no reason to come and see Franklin. Plus, he'd only once been haunted by a ghost he knew, and that had been Mama.

"I have been seeing a boy, lately," Franklin said slowly. "But I don't know if it's this Hollis or not. He hasn't told me his name, or his *intent*."

"If I came out while the ghost was there, do you think I'd be able to see him?" Preacher Sinclair asked. He sounded far too eager for Franklin's taste.

"Don't know. Don't think so," Franklin said, starting to feel stubborn. "You weren't able to see much when we was hunting the creature a few years back."

"There's a reward," Preacher Sinclair said. "For any information about their boy."

Franklin shrugged. "Wouldn't be much I could tell them if he was already dead," he said. "I don't know anything about him, like where he died or where his body is." Franklin shivered. He didn't like thinking about being haunted by ghosts that weren't properly buried. But that may have been the case with the current ghost.

"I will ask the ghost about his name, though," Franklin promised. "The next time I see him."

Preacher Sinclair sighed, then nodded. "Are you sure you don't want someone else there with you?"

"I'm sure," Franklin said. He knew that the preacher meant well. He also knew that the boy was scared. Bringing the preacher in might make the boy run. Franklin didn't know where a ghost would run to, but he didn't want to risk it.

"All right. Keep your eye out, though. Let me know if you do meet the boy, so I can at least try to prepare the parents for the worst," Preacher Sinclair said.

"I will," Franklin said. He wasn't lying. Not really. He'd keep an eye out for the boy. And he'd ask his current guest if his name was Hollis.

But Franklin didn't know what he'd do if the boy said *yes*.

CHAPTER 4

Franklin took his time riding his bike to Darryl's house for Sunday dinner. He had too much to think about, between the boy ghost and what was going on with Tommy. And Julie was gonna need more of him, too.

Luckily, he had an understanding boss. Karl didn't mind Franklin coming in late at least half the time, usually because he had a visiting ghost.

Katherinesville, like many of the towns in the area, had been built in the early 1900s, and had once been an important stop on the railroad. Downtown still had the fancy painted buildings with white trim. Streets were lined with tall shady trees. Large brick homes with wide yards made up the neighborhoods to the north of town.

Darryl lived in a newer neighborhood, east and south of town, filled with one-story houses and no sidewalks. The yards here were more open, the grass finally recovering from all the kids playing on it and the hot summer days.

Franklin leaned his bike up against the garage door when he arrived. He noticed that the boy's bikes had been put away—

maybe locked away as a punishment for disappearing? Aunt Jasmine's beat up green Ford was already parked behind Darryl's big black truck, and Julie's car was in the street. Even Jason's SUV Jeep was there.

The whole family had gathered. Franklin couldn't help but pause and be thankful for a moment.

None of them was ever going to be rich. Not in terms of money. But they were all, each and every one of them, certainly blessed.

Franklin took a deep breath, bracing himself, then let himself into the house, the loud chattering of the adults, the squealing of the kids, the abrasive noise of his family rolling over him.

No place like home.

Franklin first went into the living room, looking for Julie. She was perched on a side of the couch, where Georgia had been sitting the night before, listening to Aunt Jasmine give her more advice about being pregnant.

"Hi, beautiful," Franklin said, coming over to Julie and leaning down to kiss the top of her head. She still had that wonderful womanly smell, though Franklin also caught a scent now and again of milk. She wore a green smock-like shirt that rode high on her belly, and soft gray pants that were loose enough to fit.

"And what about me?" Aunt Jasmine asked, sitting up straighter and putting her fists on her waist, mock glaring at him.

"Now, you know I think you're beautiful, too," Franklin said, coming over to kiss her cheek.

"That's better. Now, shoo, we're talking woman things," Aunt Jasmine instructed.

"Is there anything I can get you?" Franklin asked Julie

before he let himself be chased away.

"I'm good," Julie said, holding up her lemonade.

They sometimes shared a beer now and again, though neither of them was heavy drinkers. It just tasted good.

"You let me know," Franklin told her before he moved into the next area of loud chaos, namely, the kitchen.

Darryl caught Franklin's eye as he came in, then tilted his head toward the backdoor.

Franklin nodded and after grabbing himself a beer, went out into the back.

The kids were already there. Tommy was the oldest, almost fifteen, while Jason's girls were the youngest at six and eight.

They'd separated into two camps, with the girls on one side of the shaded porch and the boys on the other side. Now, the boys were outnumbered, as there were only three of them and there were five girls. The youngest girl looked like she'd still like to go run around the yard, while the older girls held court and played with their dolls.

Franklin didn't even try to join the girls' side. He knew he'd just be shooed away if he did.

"What's up, gentlemen?" Franklin asked as he sat down near the boys.

While the girls were all rapidly talking with each other, the boys had been sitting more quiet and morose.

"Nothing," Tommy said, not meeting his eye.

"Yeah," Austin said. "We ain't talking 'bout nothing."

"Then you two wouldn't mind if Tommy and I go have a chat, right?" Franklin asked.

"What you gonna talk about?" Pete asked.

"That's between Tommy and I," Franklin said. He almost said, "between us men," but Tommy weren't there yet.

"All right," Tommy said. He sounded dejected. "Let's go talk."

Franklin took Tommy along the side of the house, past the boys' bedroom window, out to the front of the house, then back in through the front door and directly into the garage. By going that roundabout way, they wouldn't have to be passing in front of all the adults. Franklin figured that were kinder to the boy.

It was cooler in the garage than in the backyard. It smelled of grease. Franklin looked closely before he leaned against Darryl's workbench in his good Sunday suit, but it appeared clean. Cleaner than Franklin had expected. Darryl's tools were all neatly put away in the toolbox that was bigger than Franklin's dresser, or hung up on the wall above the workbench. The gun safe stood beside the bench, taller than Franklin and securely locked. It held more bows and arrows than guns, though Darryl still kept a few around.

Franklin stood there for a moment, just looking at the boy. Young man. Franklin was just six feet tall. Darryl was a hair shorter, though he'd never admit that. Tommy hadn't reached his full height yet. Franklin figured he'd be at least as tall as Darryl in another year or so, maybe even taller.

Tommy had a wide brown face and dark eyes that always looked soulful to Franklin. Though the boy had a small nose that practically melted across the rest of his face, he had a wide mouth and big lips, similar to Aunt Jasmine's. He wore his hair clipped short. He'd changed out of his church clothes and wore a basketball jersey over a pair of long shorts.

When Franklin saw the scratches on Tommy's legs, he thought for a moment of the ghost in his backyard, the scratches on his legs.

What had these children been running from? Was it the same thing?

"Now, I know your ma and pa have been asking about what happened, asking again and again," Franklin said, taking a sip of his beer. "I'm gonna tell you a story, instead."

Tommy's didn't seem to be expecting that. "Okay," he said.

"Don't know if you remember my mama," Franklin said. "She worked all her life at a beauty salon downtown. Cut your hair until she died."

"I remember," Tommy's said. He sounded resentful, as if this were yet *another* long story from some adult with no purpose whatsoever.

"You ever visit her salon?" Franklin asked. He knew that Mama used to cut the boys' hair over here, in the backyard.

"No," Tommy's said, shaking his head.

Was he lying? Franklin wasn't sure.

"So you never seen her with her deck of cards?" Franklin asked.

Tommy's blinked and looked up, honestly surprised. "No, I didn't."

"Mama had a deck like yours," Franklin said. "Blue bicycle. Didn't remember until late last night, after I'd gone to bed."

"That ain't my deck," Tommy said. "I never seen it before."

Franklin knew the boy was lying about both things.

"I don't believe you, Tommy. That deck is yours. It's part of you. At least now," Franklin said, taking another drink of his beer. He didn't like confronting the boy, but he knew he must.

"I don't know what you mean," Tommy said.

"Mama used to use her deck to tell fortunes," Franklin said. "She always said it were just for fun, something for her and the girls to do when there weren't many customers."

Tommy kept his face deliberately blank.

"Don't know what happened to her deck," Franklin said,

though he suspected that Tommy had somehow gotten ahold of it.

Tommy just glared at him, not saying anything.

"Mama had a tarot deck, too." Franklin pulled the small box from his jacket pocket and handed it to Tommy. He'd always kept it in a box in the storage shed out front. It hadn't felt right to just throw the deck away or to give it away, though he'd never used it.

Tommy stared at the cards like a drowning man staring at a rope ready to pull him out of the water. But he kept his hands clenched in fists at his sides.

"Take it," Franklin said firmly.

The boy didn't need to be told twice. He held on to the cards with both hands but stared at the ground as if he didn't dare look too closely at them.

"Mama always said that she didn't have a gift, not like me, not like Lexine," Franklin said. "But she must have seen some sort of future in the cards, at least once or twice. She knew my future, and she scared off at least one of her clients as well by being too truthful."

Tommy's head came up, finally meeting Franklin's eye. "What, you think I can do something with the cards?" he challenged.

"I don't know what you can do," Franklin said. "Why don't you show me?"

Tommy pressed his lips together as if holding back his words.

"I won't tell Darryl, or anyone else," Franklin promised. "This is just between us two. For now."

After a moment, Tommy nodded to himself. "All right."

He slid the cards out of the box, putting it on the workbench. He glanced at the deck, as if making sure he knew what it held. Then he expertly shuffled the cards in midair, not needing a solid surface to fan the cards against.

Franklin watched the tension bleeding out of the boy as he worked with the cards. His actions smoothed out.

"Here. Cut the deck," Tommy said, handing the cards to Franklin.

Franklin complied. He weren't surprised that the cards had taken on a warmth all their own.

Tommy stood up taller than he had been, his shoulders back. His eyes had taken on a fierceness that Franklin had never seen in the boy before. Despite how fat his fingers looked, they moved with an unexpected speed and grace. His voice had grown deeper as well, more calm.

"Simple lay out," Tommy—no, Tom—said, coming to stand beside Franklin at the workbench. "Past," he said, turning over the first card. "Present. Future," he announced as he put down the next two. Then he gave a long whistle.

"Two of pentacles," Tom said, pointing at a card where a funny looking man held two discs with stars on them while balancing on a seesaw on the sand. Behind him were ocean waves, with more than one ship crossing the water. "You've been working to keep a balance, between the world and the spirit, between the living and the dead."

Tom paused, then pointed to the next card. "The tower," he said. The card showed a tall stone tower on fire, with a man, a woman, and a dog falling to the ground. "This is your present. Lots of change. The old world is crumbling and the new has yet to be born."

Franklin was impressed. He hadn't expected the boy to be able to do something like this at all. But it wasn't really the boy, was it? A young man stood beside him, growing into his potential.

Tom pointed to the last card. "Death," he pronounced.

Franklin found himself taking a quick sip of his beer. "What's that mean?"

"More change?" Tom said. "I don't know. This is where I don't know. Is it near future? Far away? Does knowing it's coming change it? Why tell someone if they can't?"

Suddenly, Tom swept all the cards from the workbench, tossing the rest of the deck on the floor. "I don't know. I don't want to know. Stop talking to me." He glared at the cards before turning his mournful eyes to Franklin. "How do you make it stop, Uncle Franklin?"

"Tom, Tommy, it's okay," Franklin said, reaching for the boy, willing to draw the shaking boy in.

However, Tommy didn't want that sort of comfort, the comfort an adult could give a boy, holding him close like Franklin could protect the child from the world.

Tommy stood apart, shaking his head.

"Ma says you talk with ghosts, that you done so since you were a boy like me. But I don't want to. I don't want to see the stories in the cards."

"Can't you put the cards away?" Franklin asked. He didn't understand what the boy meant.

"I've tried. But I can hear 'em. Whispering to me. If I leave 'em outside the house, other things turn into cards. Like those cards you get in magazines. They start forming patterns. Or even the magazines themselves. The stories. I can't look away."

Franklin nodded. "I didn't want to talk with the ghosts when I was a boy. They scared me, following me everywhere at first." He shivered. "I was a little younger than you the first time the ghosts started showing up, shoving their *intent* at me, trying to get me to do things for them."

"You still see 'em, right?" Tommy said.

"I do. It's my duty to work with them. To help them to pass along," Franklin said. He peered at Tommy. "My mama, she didn't have something as strong as what you have. She could put the cards away. She just sometimes hit the truth. Sounds like there's a truth inside you just wants to be told."

"I don't want to tell it!" Tommy said. "Make it go away!"

Franklin sighed. "Son, I can't do that. No one can. This is your gift. You're gonna have to accept it."

Tommy started backing away, heading toward the door. "I don't want it," he said firmly. "I don't have to take it."

"But what if it's your duty?" Franklin asked. "What if it becomes part of your job to tell the stories in the cards?"

"Take it away," Tommy said.

"Who, me?" Franklin said. "It don't work that way. I didn't give you the gift in the first place. It came from God."

"Then He can take it back because I don't want it," Tommy said.

He turned and fled the garage.

Franklin stood, surprised. He wasn't sure what had just happened, why Tommy was so scared. Though Franklin hadn't wanted his gift at first, either. Felt it made him too different from everyone else. And the ghosts kept asking him to do things he weren't comfortable doing.

Slowly, Franklin picked up the cards that Tommy had pushed onto the ground.

He sure as hell wasn't about to tell Darryl about his son. It was the boy's responsibility to tell his pa.

How could Franklin help, though? At least Tommy could state his *intent*, as wrong as it might be.

Franklin sighed.

Family.

~

Franklin tried unsuccessfully to avoid being pulled aside by Darryl, but he didn't have a choice in the matter. Darryl practically yanked Franklin's arm out of its socket after dessert had been served, pulling him out of the dining room and into the backyard.

"So? What did Tommy say?" Darryl asked as soon as he shut the door.

The sun still had its summer bite, but the evening chill was underneath. Franklin stood in his short sleeved shirt, kind of wishing for his jacket. "Tommy didn't say much," Franklin said. He was going to try to be honest with Darryl, as much as he could.

"Boy's not saying much to anyone," Darryl complained. He paced across the backyard, short, hard steps.

"He's not doing drugs," Franklin assured Darryl. "He's not in some gang."

Darryl shot a look at Franklin. "So you do know what's going on with him."

"I wouldn't say that," Franklin said, shaking his head. He still didn't know how he could help the boy. "He's looking for his path," Franklin finally said.

"What the hell does that mean?" Darryl asked. "He's a boy—"

"Young man," Franklin interrupted. "He's on the cusp of becoming a man."

Darryl shook his head. "Don't matter. He still needs to listen to his elders." Then he gasped. "Damn it! Do you find your ma's words coming out when you don't expect it?"

"Not yet," Franklin said. "But I figure once the kids come…"

Darryl sighed, all the fight going out of him. "Yeah. The kids will change everything. Not for the worst, or the better, just different, right?"

"Right," Franklin said. Then he paused. "Tommy's growing up," he said slowly. "It's gonna take him some time to find his way. But you gave him a good foundation to build on. You just need to give him some space right now."

"Not if he's running away in the middle of the night," Darryl said, looking stubborn.

"He ain't running away, going to see some girl or some gang," Franklin said. He was trying to figure out the best way to tell Darryl to hang back without breaking any confidences with Tommy. "Look. I love y'all. You're my family. However. I still need my farm. I need to breathe. Tommy needs some space and time. But he'll come around."

"He has always wanted his own room," Darryl said. "I don't know why. Jason and me shared a room forever and it was just fine."

Franklin snorted. "You sure about that? You might want to ask Jason if he remembers it the same."

Darryl nodded. "It just that?" he asked, peering closely at Franklin as the evening shadows gathered.

Franklin wouldn't lie. "Might be a bit more. But giving him some space will help with everything else."

"He ain't gonna start talking to ghosts or doing weird things, is he?" Darryl asked.

"Would you love your boy any less if it turned out he had a gift?" Franklin asked in return.

"'Course not," Darryl protested.

"You sure?" Franklin said, pressing the point. He knew he was getting too close to the truth, but he needed Darryl to stop and actually think about this. "You and me didn't always get along when we was boys, you teasing me so much because of my gifts."

"Naw, you were just teasable, Cuz," Darryl replied with a grin. "Still are."

"That may be. But you can't stop loving your boy if he turns out to be a little different. You gotta love him more, then," Franklin said seriously.

"He's gay," Darryl said flatly.

"Don't rightly know," Franklin said. He served a few gays at the fruit and vegetable stand—two of the chefs who came regularly. They seemed the same as everyone else to him.

But Darryl didn't appear to be listening anymore to Franklin. He took a deep breath then stood up. "All right. We can deal with this. Not the end of the world." He grimaced.

Franklin shook his head. "Listen to me. I don't know if Tommy is gay. All I know is he needs some space and time to figure out who he is gonna be."

Darryl narrowed his eyes at Franklin. "Fine. I just want him to be okay, you know?"

"I know," Franklin said. He held Darryl's gaze. "You've raised him to be a good person. Now, you gotta step back and let him be his own person."

"Easier said than done, Cuz," Darryl replied. He finally seemed to accept that he just didn't know what was going on with Tommy, not now, and not for a while.

"I expect you're gonna have to remind me of this exact conversation in a dozen years or more," Franklin told Darryl seriously.

"Deal," Darryl said. He nodded. "You two headed out now?"

"Yup," Franklin said. He loved his family. Wouldn't know what to do without them.

But they was also an awful lot to take sometimes.

"I'll call later this week," Franklin assured Darryl. "See how you're holding up."

"Thanks, Cuz," Darryl said. "Will see how you're holding up, too. Nothing to be nervous about at all. Women been having babies since forever."

"Thanks," Franklin said. He probably wasn't as worried as most new fathers were. Julie was a nurse and knew how to take care of herself. She also listened to him when he told her to sit down and put her feet up and take it easy for a while.

Well, mostly.

Franklin got Julie extricated from whatever racy story she and May were giggling about and out into the car. She sat while he put his bicycle into her trunk, then slid into the passenger seat.

"Home?" she asked. She sounded tired, but Franklin knew better than to offer to drive.

"Yes, please," Franklin said.

Home. To peace and quiet.

And ghosts.

CHAPTER 5

Franklin didn't see the boy ghost on Sunday night. Either he didn't come visiting, or Franklin came home from his cousin's house too late.

In the morning, Franklin got up with his alarm, leaving Julie to sleep. She only had a week or so left to work before she'd take off and give herself more time to prepare for the baby. She said she planned on sleeping the entire two weeks before the child came, if the baby arrived on its due date. She'd already given Franklin plenty of warning that most new mothers was late.

Franklin saw to his own breakfast, taking a quick pass outside in the back to see if any other ghosts were gonna show up. Normally they only came one at a time. Since the boy hadn't showed up the night before, he wanted to check.

However, no other ghost showed up that morning. Franklin spent the time sitting on one of the white metal chairs, staring out into his fields, breathing in the quiet morning air. The day was going to be another hot one, though it was getting colder every night. The cicadas hadn't started up their chorus, so he mainly heard the soft winds rustling the dried stalks, the sparrows chirping, and the far-off sound of the trucks on the interstate.

After checking his bicycle carefully, Franklin rode off to the fruit and vegetable stand. He got there just as Karl drove up in his old truck.

"Morning," Franklin told Karl, letting him unlock the stand.

Karl yawned and said, "Morning."

Franklin wasn't gonna tease Karl about yet another hot date the night before.

At least, not yet. Not until Karl was properly awake.

They fell into their easy routine setting up the stand, bringing out the boxes they'd kept in the locked refrigerators in the back, as well as unloading the fresh vegetables that Karl had in his truck, that he'd picked up from their suppliers on the way to the stand.

By the time they were finished, the first customers were already lining up. Both Karl and Franklin had strongly considered adding a coffee service. However, that would have meant expanding the stall, and the licensing would have been a pain.

Still, given the way most of the customers still seemed to be half asleep, they figured it might end up being very popular.

When the morning rush of chefs and early shoppers had died down, Franklin finally felt he could ask Karl, "You get any sleep this weekend?"

Karl snorted and shook his head. "Not enough," he admitted. Then he gave Franklin a goofy grin. "Might want to call it in early this afternoon. Go take a nap."

"You hanging up the towel?" Franklin teased. "I thought

you had more stamina." At least that was what Karl usually bragged about.

"Not with the twins," Karl said.

Before Karl could start giving Franklin all kinds of details that he did *not* want to hear, Sheriff Thompson drove up in his brown Crown Vic.

"Morning," Sheriff Thompson said as he came walking up to the stand. His tiny suspicious eyes squinted in the sunlight. He had a big nose and generally looked serious. His brown mustache grew down around the corners of his mouth. Franklin now sometimes saw the occasional white hair against the brown, and suspected that as soon as the sheriff noticed, he plucked it out. Same with his bushy eyebrows.

"Morning, Sheriff," Franklin said.

Though the sheriff was a white man, he kept insisting that he wasn't the enemy. He made an effort to be nicer to Franklin than he was to Karl.

Then again, Franklin had kept his nose clean and never been in trouble again with the law, unlike Karl who'd been arrested a few months ago for getting rowdy in a bar.

The sheriff had a bunch of fliers in one hand, setting Franklin's back up. He didn't want to put up fliers for the sheriff, not again. The local police held an annual auction and charity ball, and Karl and Franklin had been pushed into putting up fliers for it every year.

But it weren't the right time for the charity ball. That had been at the start of summer. So what did the sheriff want them to be advertising this time?

"Wanted to know if you two would put up a couple of these here at the stand," Sheriff Thompson said, shoving the fliers across the counter.

The paper was white, with big black printing across the top.

"Have you seen me?"

"Boy missing?" Franklin asked. "That's too bad."

He stiffened when he saw the name. Hollis Chambers. The same boy that Preacher Sinclair had been asking about.

"You seen him?" the sheriff asked, his beady eyes staring hard at Franklin.

"No, sir," Franklin said automatically.

"Take a good look," Sheriff Thompson insisted, pushing the flier closer.

With a sigh, Franklin picked up one of the flier and examined the picture in the middle of it. The black and white photo was grainy, showing a young boy in three-quarter profile, standing in a living room with a TV in the background. Underneath the photo was his name, his age, and a number to call about the reward.

The amount was more than Franklin made in a year.

"Haven't seen him," Franklin said firmly, putting down the flier again. He was proud of how his hand didn't shake, how the sheriff seemed to be believing him, for once.

"Fine," Sheriff Thompson said. "You just let me know if you do, you hear me?"

"I do," Franklin said, though he weren't about to promise anything.

He weren't about to say anything either, about how it appeared that that ghost in his backyard was the same as the boy in the flier.

No matter how Sheriff Thompson would say he weren't the enemy, there was no way in hell that a black man was about to admit to knowing that a white boy, particularly a rich white boy, was dead.

FRANKLIN WAS BICYCLING BACK HOME FROM THE STAND that night when he got a call from Julie. He knew it was her calling because she'd set up a special ringtone just for her on his phone.

"Hello, darling," Franklin said, pulling over to the side of the road so he could answer. She might need him to go back to the stand and bring them something for dinner, or to go into town before he came home.

"Just calling to make sure you were on your way," Julie said. "So you can be here to entertain your guest."

"What guest?" Franklin asked, confused. One of the ghosts hadn't come into the house, had it? Julie wouldn't have been able to see it even if one did, though.

"Tommy's here," Julie said quietly. "I've already let Darryl and Georgia know he's having dinner with us. He wants to talk with you."

"I'm on my way," Franklin said, hanging up and then pedaling fast as he could the rest of the way home.

Tommy's bike was resting against the storage shed door. Franklin put both bikes inside the shed before he went into the house.

"Hi, darling," Franklin said, kissing Julie's cheek as she was standing at the stove, turning over the fish in the pan. The kitchen smelled of lemon and garlic. Then he turned and held out his hand for Tommy to shake. "Nice to see you," he said solemnly.

"You too," Tommy said. He was looking around, as if he'd never seen the place before.

"There aren't any ghosts here," Franklin told him. "The only one who's been visiting has been out back. Want to come say hello to him?"

Tommy gulped. His dark skin grew a little ashen but he

gave a determined nod.

"I'll keep dinner warm until you get back," Julie assured Franklin as he gave her arms a quick squeeze.

Franklin felt his love for her bubble up again. She'd accepted his ghosts, his duty, better than anyone else in the family since Mama and Lexine had both died.

"Thank you," Franklin said. He opened up the door leading out of the kitchen and held it open for Tommy.

Tommy gulped and walked bravely out into the yard.

"This way," Franklin said, leading the way out to the back.

The sun was just setting, the evening still. Clouds covered the sky, hiding the sunset and the stars. It would probably start raining later. Franklin didn't like riding his bike in the rain on the way to work. On the way home, it was fine. Still, they needed the rain to knock all the dust out of the air.

"Sit," Franklin said, pointing to one of the white metal chairs while he took his place on the other.

"Now what?" Tommy asked. He sat on the very edge of his seat, looking ready to leap out of it at the slightest noise.

"We wait," Franklin said. He turned his face toward the corn field and took a deep breath of the good night air. "The boy didn't come last night," Franklin warned. "So I'm hoping he comes tonight." He weren't gonna mention that the ghost might not come if there was someone else there. For the most part they weren't bothered by Julie, but every once in a while, they'd insist that Franklin talk with them on their own.

"All right," Tommy said. He stared out into the field, taking his own deep breath.

Franklin could see the night starting to settle the boy. Tommy's shoulders stopped being perched up around his ears, and his eyes started to look more relaxed.

"What's that?" Tommy suddenly said, leaping up to his feet.

"What's what?" Franklin said, leaning back. He hadn't heard anything, hadn't felt the cold that usually announced the presence of a ghost.

"Nothing," Tommy said, sitting back down. "Just…thought I heard a sigh. Like someone letting out a deep breath. You know?"

Franklin just shrugged. He hadn't heard anything at all. Yet…

A cold wind blew past Franklin's shoulder that didn't rustle any of the corn in the field. "Something's coming," Franklin said.

Tommy grew tense again.

The boy appeared. He still had that sharp look to his eyes, scared out of his skin.

"Do you see him?" Franklin asked quietly.

"No?" Tommy said, sounding unsure.

"Here," Franklin said. He reached across the small white metal table and wrapped his hand around Tommy's forearm.

"There's something there," Tommy said, shocked. "Something white, like fog. But it's person shaped!"

"There's nothing the ghost can do to you," Franklin said firmly. He'd learned that with Lexine, when they'd been sharing their difference sights. Lexine learned to see a ghost like Franklin could, but she could never hear them, couldn't feel their *intent*.

"Wow," Tommy said after a moment. He tossed a grin at Franklin. "Kinda creepy, but kinda cool."

Franklin felt a wash of pride. Maybe he wasn't as uncool as the rest of the adults were.

"Evening," Franklin said when the ghost finally seemed to notice the pair of them there. The boy's eyes darted from Franklin to Tommy and back, but he didn't disappear.

"It's gonna be all right," Franklin told the ghost, as he had every night.

The boy just shook his head.

"You can believe Uncle Franklin," Tommy told the ghost. "He don't lie."

That seemed to impress the ghost. Was that because Tommy was just a few years older than the ghost, not an adult?

"What's your name?" Franklin asked after the ghost had turned away from them to stare out at the field. He looked more hungry tonight. Maybe it was getting time for him to pass on.

The ghost didn't say anything.

"Is it Hollis Chambers?" Franklin said after a bit.

The ghost turned back to look at Franklin. He looked puzzled at first. Then understanding dawned in his eyes. He nodded. It was like he'd forgotten his own name until Franklin said it.

Then the ghost started shaking all over, shivering something fierce. He threw back his head to scream, a silent yell that tightened all the muscles in his throat, his hands clenched in fists.

Franklin felt his heart breaking at the sight of the boy's rage. He weren't scared now.

"What happened to you?" Franklin asked as the boy finished his yelling.

Hollis looked at Franklin, then at Tommy, shook his head, and disappeared.

"What does that mean?" Tommy asked Franklin.

"I haven't a clue."

∾

"You can't tell anyone that you saw the ghost of Hollis Chambers," Franklin told Tommy seriously. They'd just finished dinner and were eating some of the peach cobbler that Aunt Jasmine had sent home with them, leftover from Sunday dinner.

"I know," Tommy said. "They'd think you killed him or something stupid."

"Yup," Franklin said.

"But you gotta help him, Uncle Franklin," Tommy said. "He's scared."

"That's right," Franklin said. "I gotta do my duty. Just like you might have a duty that you're gonna have to do."

Tommy looked stubborn for a bit. "But it'll make me different," he said after a moment.

"Different isn't always bad," Julie said quietly, reaching across the table to give Franklin's arm a warm squeeze.

"Your cousins will tease you," Franklin told him seriously. "But you're growing up into a fine young man. You can stand a little teasing."

"As for everyone else in town?" Julie said. "They don't matter."

Tommy snorted, obviously not believing them.

"All right, they do matter," Julie said. "But in the end, it's just your family who counts."

Franklin knew they weren't gonna to change Tommy's mind anytime soon. But they'd at least given him something to think about.

"How do you find your ghosts?" Tommy asked as Julie was driving Tommy home. Franklin rode along in the backseat, keeping them both company.

"They find me," Franklin told him. "I don't go looking for them, that's for damned sure."

Tommy shook his head. "The stories…They find me. But I don't always know who they belong to."

"Do you need to collect them up until you run into the right people?" Franklin asked. He weren't sure how the boy's gift would work.

Tommy shrugged. "Don't know."

"At some point, you're gonna have to tell your ma and pa about your gift," Franklin said again.

Tommy nodded. "I will. Just…not yet."

Franklin weren't sure what the boy was waiting for. However, he wasn't gonna push.

Plants, ghosts, and people all came into their own on their own schedule, not on his.

"You let me know if you see Hollis again," Tommy said as he got out of the car. "I just—you let me know."

"I will," he promised as he climbed up out of the backseat, stretching his legs for a moment and breathing in the cool night air.

Tommy stuck out his hand to shake Franklin's. "Thank you, Uncle Franklin," Tommy said seriously. "For showing me. For not pushing me." He paused and grinned, his white teeth bright in his dark face. "At least, not too much."

"You're welcome," Franklin said, giving the young man's hand a firm shake. "You'll do the right thing."

"So will you," Tommy said.

The door to the house opened, bright light spilling into the evening. Tommy squared up his shoulders and marched toward his parents standing there, worried.

"He's gonna be all right," Franklin said as he slid back into the car, sitting in the front seat next to Julie.

He knew they weren't outta the woods yet. But maybe Tommy would talk to Darryl and Georgia now.

And even if he wouldn't tell them, not yet, he at least had some people in the family who he could talk with.

~

THE NEXT NIGHT JULIE WAS WORKING LATE AGAIN, SO Franklin made himself a sandwich before he went out to see his ghost. It had rained hard most of the day, and the night had a chill. A lot of colorful gourds filled the front of the stand. Pumpkins, too.

Franklin and Karl were sponsoring a carving contest. They'd debated for a long time, as they'd have to give out a good prize, and that would cost them money. Plus, they had to print up fliers and buy an ad in the local weekly paper.

However, anyone who wanted to enter the contest had to buy a pumpkin from them and not one of the big chain supermarkets. They'd printed up stickers to mark their pumpkins.

It had been a lot of work, but Karl had been right, and it had brought more people to the stand, parents with kids who generally bought a little bit more than just the pumpkin.

Karl and Franklin had been extra nice to anyone new, hoping that they'd start coming back regular like.

Franklin brought a towel with him that night so he could dry off the white metal chair before he sat down. The chill bit right through his jeans. More rain was predicted for tomorrow. Clouds covered the sky, hiding the stars. The pond next door, in Mrs. Averson's empty fields, hadn't come back yet. It would though, in the next few days probably, and Franklin would start hearing frogs again, at least until it got too cold.

What would happen with Tommy and his gift? What kinds of stories would he collect? Would it just be about strangers, like with Franklin and his ghosts? Could someone change a future they knew about?

And what had that reading meant for Franklin? There was death in his future. But hell, there was death in everyone's future, eventually. That was just part of the natural order of things. He hadn't told Julie about Tommy's reading, hadn't wanted her worrying about it.

The baby would be fine, he told himself again. Women had healthy babies all the time.

But sometimes they had unhealthy ones, a worry that Franklin just couldn't shake.

Finally, as the night was settling in and Franklin was considering getting up and going back inside the warm house, he felt a rush of goosebumps across his shoulders and up his neck that told him that a ghost had arrived.

"Evening," Franklin said as a mist sprang up out of nowhere right in front of him.

He frowned. That seemed like an awful lot of light and fog for just the boy.

The mist split, and now two ghosts stood in front of Franklin.

"Howdy," Franklin said, nodding his head to the newcomer, though he felt his heart sinking down to the bottoms of his shoes.

It was another young boy.

The pair of them held hands. The newcomer was a bit shorter than Hollis, though if Franklin had to guess, they was both about the same age. It was another white boy.

And—damn it!—he weren't dressed in his best suit either, but in shorts and a T-shirt.

His legs was all scratched to hell, too.

Since Mama had stopped haunting Franklin, he'd only been

seeing one ghost at a time. He weren't sure why they was all taking turns.

Or why these two showed up together.

"Can you tell me your name?" Franklin asked the new boy.

He didn't seem as scared as Hollis had been. No, he seemed quite angry instead. He burned with a brighter light than Hollis.

The name came through loud and clear. *Andrew.*

"Nice to meet you, Andrew," Franklin said.

The three of them just breathed in the night air for a few moments. Franklin wanted to get back inside his warm house, but he made himself wait. Was there something else the boys wanted to tell him?

"It's gonna be all right," Franklin said after a bit, repeating the words he'd said to Hollis every night since the boy had started showing up.

Hollis shook his head, like he always did.

Andrew peered at Franklin like he didn't understand the words. Or maybe he just didn't believe them. Then Andrew pointed at the empty chair, the one that Tommy had been in the other night.

The *intent* wasn't clear. Franklin just got a feeling of curiosity from the boy.

"Where's Tommy?" Franklin asked, trying to make sure he understood.

Andrew nodded.

Is that why Hollis had brought Andrew? So he could meet Tommy? Did it have something to do with Tommy's gift? Did he need to tell the fortunes of these two? That didn't make no sense. The only future they had was to step out of this world and on to the next.

"I don't know where he is right now," Franklin lied. He

weren't exactly sure why he didn't want to tell the truth to these ghosts.

Maybe he didn't want them to go haunting Tommy and Darryl. Though he wasn't sure what harm it could bring. Most people couldn't see the ghosts, couldn't feel them, not unless they walked right through them.

Andrew pointed again at the chair beside Franklin. He wanted Tommy there, in that chair. Now.

"I'll see if I can fetch him," Franklin said. He couldn't promise that Tommy would come. "I'll try to bring him tomorrow night. All right?"

Andrew shook his head. He wanted Tommy here. Right now.

Hollis shook their joined hands, getting Andrew to look at him. They stared at each other for a moment.

Even Gloria and Mama hadn't seemed to talk much to each other when they'd both been haunting him. Franklin weren't surprised that they didn't say anything out loud. Ghosts couldn't make any noises.

Yet, it still seemed to Franklin that the boys had communicated, saying something to each other, something urgent and yet sad.

After another few moments, both ghosts disappeared suddenly, unlike how they'd arrived.

Franklin had a bad feeling about this. Should he warn Tommy that a ghost might be coming to see him? Should he tell Darryl?

It felt like an unnecessary worry. Franklin didn't know for certain. And he hated saying anything when he didn't know.

Still, he called Darryl anyway, to see if the boy could come over for dinner again the following day.

CHAPTER 6

THIS TIME, TOMMY SEEMED MORE READY TO MEET Franklin's ghosts. He admitted that he hadn't told his parents about being able to see the future in the cards, not yet.

Franklin had made them both fried egg sandwiches, with peanut butter this time, as well as a side of greens. He'd been eating a lot healthier since Julie had moved in. Particularly since she pointed out that if he wanted to set a good example for their own kid, he'd have to eat everything on his plate. Every time.

At least Tommy didn't seem to mind eating his greens too much. After dinner, he sat out back behind the house with Franklin, sipping sweet tea and watching the night take over the fields.

"You know, I always thought it would make me crazy to live way out here," Tommy admitted after a few minutes. "I was going to move to Louisville or something after high school. Maybe even Atlanta. Get away from all…this."

"All this peace and quiet?" Franklin asked.

"Yeah. It's just too quiet sometimes, you know?"

Franklin shook his head. As he'd gotten older, he'd found he wanted the quiet more, not less. "This land just lets me be," Franklin said after a bit. "Gives me space and time to breathe."

"I think I understand," Tommy said after a bit. "But I know this would get to me after a while."

"To each their own," Franklin said. He actually figured that Tommy was right. At least for him. Both Franklin and Lexine needed someplace isolated to do their work with ghosts and spirits. Tommy, though, would be working more with the living than with the dead. He needed to be someplace where he might run into someone needing his gift.

The sun firmly set and the night grew chilly. Franklin was glad that he'd insisted both he and Tommy come out here with jackets on. A mist rose up across the fields, about a foot high and wispy, like a blanket covering the roots. Mr. Wilkerson up the road had a fire going again, though the air also smelled like more rain coming.

Tommy had brought the cards with him, both the tarot deck that Franklin had left out on the table for Tommy to pick up, along with the other set, the one that Darryl and Franklin had found wedged between the two fence boards.

"Where did you get the bicycle deck?" Franklin asked Tommy as he carefully placed both decks on the table between them.

Tommy shrugged. "I think we've always had them," he said. "They were just sitting on the shelf in the game closet, with the puzzles."

Franklin knew the place Tommy was referring to. The kids had gone through a long phase of playing board games and putting together jigsaw puzzles, and so a closet had been dedicated to holding the boxes. It was curious though, that there had been a set of cards tucked away on those shelves. No one in the family played card games, Aunt Jasmine and Mama not being part of any bridge gang.

Had they at one time been the cards Mama used to tell fortunes with? Franklin couldn't rightly say, not without asking Mama. And she were finally resting peacefully.

He hoped she'd be proud of him, happy for the family.

"I don't remember when I picked 'em up and started carrying them around," Tommy said as he held the deck, looking at the cards. "Just put them in my backpack one day. Carried them for a long time before I ever pulled them out and used them."

"How do you tell stories with them?" Franklin asked, curious. He could see how to use the tarot deck—it was full of pictures, not just numbers and suits.

Tommy gave him a big grin. "The different suits are like the tarot suits. Hearts are water, like cups. Diamonds mean earth, like the pentacles. And so on. I looked up what each card meant in an old book I found in the library, but it didn't make any sense. I need to listen to the cards themselves, not what someone else thinks."

"I understand," Franklin said. Everything he'd ever read about ghosts didn't jive with what he did almost every day, dealing with them.

Tommy put down the regular cards and picked up the tarot deck. "I've been looking at these online. Looking at the major and minor arcana. But I never seen an actual deck before."

"You're welcome to keep those," Franklin said.

"Thanks, Uncle Franklin," Tommy said as he fanned out the cards. Even in the dim light of the evening, he seemed to be able to see the face of each and every card. He was nodding his head as he looked, as if the cards was talking to him, a silent conversation between new friends, telling each other their secrets.

A chill washed over Franklin. "The ghosts are coming," he warned the boy.

"Bring 'em," Tommy said. He held up the deck of cards like it was a weapon.

Both Andrew and Hollis arrived at the same time. They appeared a little more substantial tonight, and Hollis had regained some of what Franklin would call a normal ghostly glow, not looking so dim.

The boys still held hands, as if they were afraid to let go, some kind of lifeline between them.

"Evening, boys," Franklin said, greeting the ghosts.

They looked at Franklin, then at Tommy.

"Can you seem 'em?" Franklin asked Tommy.

"I see a mist," Tommy said, staring hard into the darkness. "No faces or bodies."

Franklin reached across the table and wrapped his hand around Tommy's warm arm. "Now?"

Tommy gave a quick intake of breath. "Yeah. I see them. Better tonight than before."

Andrew was staring hard at Tommy, but Franklin didn't hear him say nothing. Was the ghost trying to push his *intent* at Tommy?

"What's he saying?" Franklin asked after a bit.

"I don't know," Tommy admitted. "It's like...I can hear a wind. Almost like a storm's brewing. But I don't hear any words. We know what they want though, right?"

"Probably," Franklin said. Likely they wanted their fortunes told, though Franklin didn't know what good that would do.

"Andrew," Franklin said, trying to get the boy's attention. "Andrew, what do you and Hollis want?"

Finally, the *intent* came clear.

They wanted Tommy to read the cards. Not the playing deck, but the tarot cards.

"They want their fortune from the tarot deck," Franklin relayed.

"Okay," Tommy said. He picked up the cards and started shuffling them. Even in the dim light Franklin could see the change in the boy, how he sat up straighter, how his movements all smoothed out.

Franklin's hand, still resting on Tommy's arm, grew warm. Huh. Franklin kinda wished that when he saw a ghost or worked with them that he might get warm, too.

Tommy fanned the cards out in his hand. "Pick one," he instructed Andrew.

Franklin watched, curious what the ghost would do. No ghost he knew of was strong enough to be able to draw a card. They couldn't move physical stuff. They had to have a mighty power to affect the living.

That didn't mean the ghosts didn't sometimes knock over Franklin's corn. Some ghosts were just angry enough and mean enough to be able to do that.

Andrew didn't try to draw a card out, though. Instead, with a single finger, he touched one of the cards on the far side of the spread.

Tommy shivered. How much of the cold of the ghost had just transferred itself to the boy?

Franklin was gonna have to make them both some hot chocolate after this.

Tommy cut the deck, using the card that Andrew selected as the top card.

"Three card spread," Tommy said, "past, present, and future."

Franklin let go of Tommy's arm as he turned, laying the cards out on the table.

A familiar card came up. "The tower," Tommy said as he laid it down. The picture of the tower with people being thrown out of it, lightning across the sky and fire everywhere. "The world changed for you. You were thrown out of your life forcibly, made to move on, against your will."

Franklin looked at the ghosts, but he didn't get a reading out of them. It was like they was holding themselves still, bracing themselves for what came next.

"Nine of swords," Tommy said as he placed down the next card. It showed a woman in her bed, hands over her face. Nine swords hung from the wall behind her. Carved into the base of the bed showed a duel, maybe of the woman and her fiercest foe. "Regret," he said. "Got a lot of sadness there. Every time you think about the past. There's nothing but hurt."

Tommy—no, Tom—looked up and spoke directly to the ghosts instead of to the cards. "That's the present. It also means you're stuck here. No looking forward. Nothing to move on to. Too much regret holding you back."

The ghosts didn't nod in agreement, or disagree, either. They seemed to be absorbing every word Tom told them, holding it deep inside them like a warm light.

"Seven of staves," Tom said as he drew the last card. It showed a man on a hill, holding a long stick and defending himself from six other sticks rising up to attack him. "Conflict," Tom said. "Battle. A fight to maintain even the position you have." He sighed.

"See him?" Tom continued, pointing at the man defending his position. "He's wearing two different shoes. It's like he can't decide what he's really doing. Is he coming or going? Staying here and defending this hill, or giving up and moving on?"

Tom turned to face the ghosts again. "You're in a hard place. But you're divided. You won't get anywhere until you figure out what you're doing. Staying here and fighting? Or moving on?" He gestured to the field behind the ghosts.

Could Tom see the open space where the ghosts usually went to? Where they moved on?

The ghosts looked at each other. Again, they was silently talking. Fighting, probably. They was still boys.

"It's gonna be all right," Franklin assured the two ghosts, as he did every time.

Fear returned to Hollis. Franklin saw it grow in his eyes. His light dimmed. He cast a look of longing over his shoulder, staring at the field.

Franklin knew the boy wanted to move on. He weren't quite ready yet, but he'd started considering it, at any rate.

Andrew had a lot of fight left in him, though. He still had something to settle here on earth.

"What happened to you boys?" Franklin asked quietly. He didn't know if there was anything he could do for them.

Hollis and Andrew looked hard at each other again. They seemed to come to some agreement and they both disappeared abruptly.

"What was that all about?" Tom asked, his voice still carrying a man's overtones.

"I'm not sure," Franklin said. "I think your reading gave them something to think about."

Tom shook his head. "It isn't just them, Uncle Franklin. There are others."

"What do you mean?" Franklin asked, alarmed. "Other boys? That been killed? Taken out of their life before their time?"

Tom nodded slowly. "Yes," he said. His voice sounded far away. "Not an army's worth. But more than a few."

"Too many," Franklin said firmly. Even one was too many.

"Yes," Tom said, his voice taking on a whisper. He gathered up the cards and reverently put them back into their box. "Too many. And they don't know how to stop him. But I think…I think they're gonna try."

After Julie had gone to bed, Franklin stayed up for a while, sitting on the couch, drinking more hot chocolate and thinking. Rain had started again, pattering softly on the roof. The fresh plastic smell of the baby toys made Franklin want to open a window, but it was just too cold outside. Soft blue fabric covered the loveseat—some kind of micro-suede—that was stain and water proof, something they'd need in the coming days.

Franklin didn't know what to make of Tom's predictions. He knew that Tom weren't lying. Someone was out there, killing boys, taking away their chance to become young men.

But was it someone? Or something?

Franklin was comfortable dealing with a monster or a creature. Something that someone had conjured. He'd dealt with powers beyond human reckoning for most of his life.

What if it was just a man? A twisted soul, doing the devil's work without no prompting?

How the hell would Franklin be able to combat that? He couldn't tell the police. They wouldn't believe him. A black man would be too easy a target, particularly since the victims was white boys.

Who would have access to the boys? Was it a school

teacher? Schools was too dangerous already, with kids going in with guns and shooting them up. (Every time something like that happened, Franklin had troubles sleeping for a week, worrying about someone coming and shooting up one of the local schools, killing someone in his family.)

Darryl was one of those who refused to register his guns. He claimed it weren't no goddamn business of the governments. Particularly as a black man.

Then again, Darryl ridiculed anyone who needed to own a machine gun, or anything that was either semi- or fully-automatic. They weren't good for hunting, not unless you was that piss poor of a shot. And even then, you'd blow your prey to pieces and what good was that when it came time to put food on the table?

Could it be a preacher? Franklin shook his head, unwilling to go down that rabbit hole. He weren't no police detective. He knew that there had to be a connection between the boys, between Hollis and Andrew. And the others.

How could Franklin stop this monster, even if it were just a man? How could he even find him?

TWO DAYS LATER, FRANKLIN STILL DIDN'T HAVE AN ANSWER. Neither Andrew or Hollis had come back though. Were they trying to convince whatever other boys remained here as ghosts to join them in fighting the monster?

Franklin spent every evening sitting in his backyard, even with the rain, hoping they'd come by, but they never did.

As no other ghosts had stepped in, Franklin wasn't optimistic that either Hollis or Andrew had moved on.

Finally they got a break in the rain, and the day dawned

sunny and clear. It wasn't warm, even in the sunlight. However, the chill in the air made Franklin want to try something.

So on his break that day, Franklin went to the library, looking up all that he could find on Hollis. Seemed the boy was kinda quiet and shy, as well as well liked in school. Police couldn't find any evidence of a struggle. The boy had been riding his bike home and never made it. They found the bike along Ellis Street, just tossed to the side like a careless boy might.

What would get Hollis to stop? To drop his bike that way?

Franklin didn't rightly know, but he decided he'd take his own cruise up that way after he left the library.

Ellis Street was in the northern part of town, with the fancy houses made of brick. Most of 'em had more than one chimney, used originally for keeping the house warm. Franklin would also bet they had more than one entrance too, one for the white folks and one for the servants. The yards were still green, with gardeners coming in and blowing off any leaf that dared fall on them. Cool winds blew through the trees, sending shivers up Franklin's spine, despite the sweat he'd been working up with all this riding.

The neighborhoods up here was peaceful, most people gone off to work and the kids at school. Expensive cars that all looked brand new were parked in the driveways, mainly SUVs. Sidewalks here weren't in much better shape than most of Katherinesville, with broken concrete from where the tree roots had popped up. It made it hard to ride his bike along, even slowly.

The streets were in better condition. Looked like most of the potholes got fixed when they showed up, instead of waiting until they got big enough to swallow a sportscar whole. The curbs were all new too, white concrete with proper gutters and drains going down into the sewers.

There wouldn't be any rats in those sewers, or at least not big enough to carry away a child.

Franklin shook his head as he drove his bike out onto the street. He shouldn't be watching late night movies. Gave him all kinds of ideas he just didn't need.

A tinkling sound came over Franklin's shoulder. It sounded like the bells playing the tune was warped. He couldn't figure out what it was. Had he passed a church over a couple of blocks?

Finally, Franklin found a driveway to pull into and turn around.

A bright pink truck was slowly coming up the street. Colorful polka dots had been painted across the grill, then up above the windshield. A huge, old-fashioned speaker sat on the top of the truck like a metal bullhorn, playing the off-tune music.

A large white man sat behind the wheel. He had on glasses, magnifying his eyes, making them seem as big as a cartoon character's. The top of his head was balding, but he had long white hair hanging on for dear life along the sides. His nose was smushed flat, as if it'd been broken once and never wanted to poke itself up again. His gray uniform stretched tight across his chest, like it was at least two sizes too small. He must have weighed over two hundred pounds, all of it fat.

He drove past Franklin as if he didn't see him, not bothering to slow down. Then again, Franklin hadn't even waved at it.

Pictures of ice cream cones, popsicles, soda pop, and popcorn decorated the side of the truck. There was a large window running across it as well.

Wasn't it kinda late in the season for an ice cream truck to be making its rounds? Then again, it was a beautiful sunny day. Maybe the truck had just decided to do one last round.

Franklin had never seen one of the trucks come out to the farm when he'd been a boy. There weren't any other kids on the lane where he'd lived, not enough customers, he suspected. Plus, Mama wouldn't have spent the money on those sorts of treats.

He had seen them coming down the main street of town, particularly on a hot day in the summertime, getting business from the tourists who were aimlessly wandering around.

The music gained pitch as it passed by, the tune seeming right for just a moment, then it faded down as the truck continued on its way, sounding more somber in the lower pitch.

Just up the street the truck stopped. Two boys, also on bikes, had waved it down. They casually dropped their bikes on the sidewalk as they walked over to the truck.

Franklin had to swallow down the bile raising in his throat.

Who'd suspect an ice cream man and his truck? However, it sure would be an easy way to bring an unsuspecting boy to him. Call him around to the back of the vehicle, saying you had an extra treat for him. Then just grab him.

Franklin shook his head. There weren't no way he could prove any of that. Even if any of it were true and not just his imagination.

Slowly, Franklin walked his bike up the street. He couldn't hear the words the old man was saying to the boys over the damned tinkling music of the truck.

The boys didn't seem scared, though the old man didn't look happy. He seemed impatient, as if he couldn't wait for them to make up their minds about what they wanted.

Before Franklin pulled up even with the truck, the old man disappeared inside.

Just an arm appeared a moment later, shoving the treats at the boys. They had to step closer, the smaller one having to go up on his toes to reach his ice cream.

The truck slid away before Franklin could get any closer. The boys walked over closer to their bikes as they ate their treats.

"Howdy, boys," Franklin said as he walked up. They were dressed for the season, the older one with a red flannel shirt and jeans, the other with a black coat on over his green T-shirt.

As they seemed warry, Franklin told them, "My name's Franklin Kanly. Didn't I see you last week, at the fruit and vegetable stand up on the highway? I work there." They didn't look familiar, but since they was local, they'd know the stand.

"Maybe," said the red shirt.

"Does that ice cream truck come by here often?" Franklin asked. "He pulled away before I could get any."

"Mr. Orville comes here maybe every other week," the red shirt volunteered. "Even in the winter, when it's nice.

"But he don't like to serve your kind," the other boy said.

"Oh, really?" Franklin asked, not surprised, but a bit disgusted.

"No, not 'cause you're black. Mr. Orville don't like adults," red shirt clarified. "He makes them stand way back, give the money to the kids, and will only serve them."

"I see," Franklin said. "Only likes seeing kids, huh."

"I don't think he *likes* kids," the other boy said. "He's always mad about something."

"Why's that?" Franklin asked.

Both boys shrugged. They seemed used to the mysterious ways of adults.

"Well, I'll try and find him later," Franklin told the boys. "Thank you for your time."

"Sure thing," the kids said.

Franklin paused, then turned back to them. "You wouldn't either of you know Hollis Chambers?"

They shook their heads. "Didn't know him. He wasn't in our school," red shirt said. "But it's why we're riding together. Our mom was *freaked* that he just disappeared like that. On this road, too."

"It's good you two stick together, then," Franklin said firmly. "That's a smart idea."

He walked a little ways up the sidewalk, then stood there as the boys finished their treats and rode away together. He figured they were brothers, with red shirt being the older one. Someone had put the fear of god into them though, as they were riding side by side away, not letting each other out of sight.

Franklin was just about to ride away when a chill passed over his shoulders, announcing the appearance of a ghost.

Hollis appeared where the boys had been. He looked more angry than scared for once. He stomped his feet in place, as if trying to ruin the grass there.

His *intent* rolled over Franklin.

He weren't mad at the boys, no, he *hated* the ice cream man. Mr. Orville.

He were tied up in Hollis' death.

"Was he the one who killed you?" Franklin asked, afraid to hear the answer.

Slowly, Hollis nodded.

Find him. Hurt him. Kill him.

Franklin took a deep breath, his skin feeling sticky suddenly as Hollis's *intent* brushed past him.

No ghost could make Franklin do something against his will.

Things died. People died. All the time. That was the natural course of things.

Franklin weren't no killer. He didn't hurt people either, not on purpose.

But he was gonna stop that white man from taking more white boys.

He just didn't have a clue how to even start.

CHAPTER 7

SINCE FRANKLIN HAD A LITTLE BIT OF TIME BEFORE HE needed to return to the vegetable stand after going up to Ellis Street, he rode to the library to see what he could find about the ice cream truck and Mr. Orville.

The long row of internet computers was mostly empty. An older man sat on the very end. Though they had that orange privacy screen on them, Franklin still could see that the gentleman was looking up gardening articles.

Franklin didn't have time to point him toward the best ones. Then again, he didn't know if the man was looking up how to grow popping corn or something else.

After a little bit of searching, Franklin found the business registry for the ice cream truck. He felt like a regular detective for having even thought of it.

However, the registration for the business listed a local post office box, no home address.

On a whim, Franklin did a search on Mr. Orville. He didn't know the man's first name, so he did a search on Orville's ice cream and Kentucky.

After all the advertisements for that fake popping corn, Franklin finally found something interesting.

Mr. Orville drove a school bus in the off season, when he wasn't driving the ice cream truck.

The article wasn't about that, though. Seemed that Mr. Orville had lost his only child a while back. Boy had been a teenager, and killed himself in a car crash. The boy had been texting and driving, at least according to the newspaper, which then had a big column on why this was so dangerous.

Franklin vowed to not let any of his children have one of those dumb smartphones until they was at least twenty, if then.

However, that was the only thing that Franklin could find. No address. No phone number. Nothing that would lead Franklin to the man.

What was he gonna do now?

FRANKLIN DIDN'T KNOW WHO TO TURN TO.

Darryl would come up with some hairbrained scheme that was likely to throw them both in jail for a good long time.

Preacher Sinclair would want to know more details, all the while trying to figure out how he could go and collect the reward offered for the dead boy and use it for the church.

Sheriff Thompson was out of the question. He'd probably just arrest Franklin on principle.

Franklin knew he should tell Julie, even though he didn't want to worry her. They was married, so she couldn't be made to testify against him. He figured the TV shows got that right. That didn't mean Sheriff Thompson might not throw her into jail as well, despite the fact that the baby was coming.

He would tell her everything, just...later. He'd asked for her to trust him, and that meant he had to trust her as well.

The only person he could think to go talk to was Tommy. He weren't sure what Tommy could do with the information. Could he figure out the ice cream man with his cards? Find 'em? Or did Franklin have to go talk with Darryl about that, hunting down these monsters?

Franklin rode slowly back to the fruit and vegetable stand, getting there just as the rain started in again.

"You doing okay?" Karl asked as Franklin tipped water out of the front awning between customers. "You seem quiet today. Everything all right with the baby?"

"Everything's fine," Franklin assured Karl. He paused, then told his partner some of the truth. "It's that missing boy."

"Ah," Karl said, nodding. He was wearing a gold-and-black plaid flannel shirt over his usual black T-shirt. He grew his brown hair down to the tops of his shoulders, and had a trimmed, thin mustache. His keen eyes and sharp nose reminded Franklin of one of those old-timey generals from the Civil War, but luckily, Karl was much more than that.

"You're worried cause you got a kid of your own coming," Karl said.

"True enough," Franklin said. How could he protect his own young'uns from the monsters in the world?

"There's not much you can do besides love 'em and let 'em know you're proud of them," Karl said wisely. "And show 'em the back side of your hand when you need to."

"You ever gonna have kids?" Franklin asked, curious.

Karl shrugged. "Gotta find me as nice a lady as you got."

"Hard task," Franklin said. "Near impossible."

Karl nodded, then he narrowed his eyes and stared hard at Franklin. "I think there's something more going on with you," he said after a moment. "It's that Hollis boy. Now, I do *not* want to know if he's been haunting you. Really, Franklin. Do not tell me about that."

"Okay," Franklin said, a little confused by Karl's insistence.

"If you have been seeing that boy, that means he's been killed, and probably by something nasty. Which means you're gonna have to go after it." Karl sighed. "I don't want to lose my business partner. You make me a better man by competing as hard as you do. Make me wanna be better."

"Thank you," Franklin said. "And the same for you." The pair of them still competed every year to win the Kentucky State Fair blue ribbon award for growing the best popping corn. Neither of them had won that year—a fourteen year old had lucked into it, though Franklin had finally come away with second prize and Karl had ranked a mere fifth.

"That being said, you just let me know if you need an alibi or anything," Karl said. He gave Franklin a grin. "Hell, I'd be happy to have another fight with you if that's what it took to convince the police that you were with me."

"That's a mighty generous offer," Franklin concluded. It was as good as he'd get from anyone in his family.

"So don't tell me what you're doing," Karl repeated. "Just let me know if I can help."

"I will," Franklin said. He held out his hand for Karl to shake. Karl gripped it with a firm grip and a grim smile.

What more could Franklin ask for in a partner?

Mr. Horton—Julie's father, who always insisted that Franklin call him Bill—and the other Mr. Horton—Julie's uncle Henry—were coming over for dinner the next night.

Franklin got off work early to go help Julie with the cooking, or rather, to give her moral support while she did the lion's share of the work.

He tried helping. He truly did. She just wouldn't let him do much beyond chopping up some of the vegetables. He always did the dishes, however. It was a point of pride with him that in the two years they'd been living together, she'd never washed a single dish.

Julie's mom had disappeared out of her life when she'd been six. Franklin didn't know why the former Mrs. Horton had left. Julie heard from her occasionally, like on Christmas, or frequently a month or so after her birthday, if her ma remembered.

Franklin had never met the former Mrs. Horton. Julie had invited her to the wedding, but even though she'd RSVP'ed, she'd never showed up. She did send a one hundred dollar bill in a card that arrived three months later. With the baby coming, Franklin didn't anticipate seeing Mrs. Horton anytime soon. Seemed she didn't care much for babies or children, at least according to Julie.

The rain had held off while Franklin was peddling home from the vegetable stand. Gray clouds covered the sky, pressing down on him. Cold winds blew from the north. It weren't gonna get sunny again anytime soon. They didn't get much snow down in that part of Kentucky, just a lot of wet and cold during the winter, the kind that sank into a body and never let go.

Franklin hadn't been seeing any ghosts in his backyard, not for a few days. He'd invited Tommy to come over again, but the boy had some sort of school event going on. Instead, they'd planned on Franklin and Julie coming over to the house on Friday night. Tommy was gonna tell Georgia and

Darryl about being different, and he wanted his Uncle Franklin there.

Mr. Horton's—Bill's—zooped-up Ford Ranger already sat in the driveway by the time Franklin arrived. That meant they was early, very early. At least an hour or so.

Had something gone wrong? But Julie hadn't texted Franklin or tried to call him. He checked his phone as he put his bike away in the shed. It was charged, something he'd gotten good at, making it a habit to plug it in every night. Regular signal, no missed calls.

Still, Franklin approached the door with caution. He didn't see Sweet Bess around. Would she warn him about human monsters?

The kitchen smelled of oregano and garlic, as well as tomato sauce and bread. All of it was fresh, hell, some of it was even organic, a line that Karl and Franklin were expanding at the fruit and vegetable stand.

Julie stood at the stove, stirring up something that smelled divine. Both of the Mr. Hortons sat at the kitchen table. All the lights was on, so Franklin couldn't mistake them for ghosts.

Still, a quick pang went through him, a brief moment where he missed Mama.

She sure would have been proud of him.

Bill Horton had been a mechanic all his life. He lived and breathed cars, gear ratios, engine capacity, intakes and outputs. He was a short man with a barrel chest and stubby fingers that worked miracles with anything mechanical. His hair was just starting to go gray around the edges, and for all the softness of his jaw, he was as hard as the metal he worked with.

Henry worked as an assistant deputy for the sheriff in the next county over. He looked softer than Bill, and as far as Franklin could tell, spent most of his time in the office, not on the street. All hat and no cattle. Like his brother, he had brown hair and round features. Unlike Bill though, Franklin was pretty sure there weren't no metal underneath.

They both wore nice shirts that buttoned, jeans and boots. Both had been divorced, Bill once, Henry twice, and was looking for wife number three.

"Evening Bill. Henry," Franklin said, nodding in their direction as he walked straight over to Julie and kissed her on the cheek. "How you doing?" he asked her directly. "Should you be standing and cooking?"

Julie gave him a grin. "I'm fine. Now shoo. You three go talk out in the living room while I work my magic."

"Yes, ma'am," Franklin said. He saw the worry lines around her eyes. He didn't know what was causing her stress. He'd be happy to kick her father and uncle out of the house before they caused her any undue strain. "You sure I can't get you something?"

Julie shook her head no, but she gave him a grateful smile.

He figured he'd hear about it later, after the dinner guests left.

"You heard the lady," Franklin informed his guests, gesturing with his arm that they should mosey along further into the house.

"We was just joking," Henry said. He looked a little put out. Bill seemed indifferent. Franklin wondered if he was hiding his anger at his brother.

"Gentlemen," Franklin said slowly when they didn't look like they was gonna move. He gave them both a look that told them just how little he was amused by their antics.

"Fine, fine," Bill said, standing up first. "We can tell when we're not wanted someplace. Come on, Henry."

Henry stood up slowly and took another large swig of his beer, finishing it.

Franklin stood there like a solid wall between Julie and her relatives as Henry walked over to the refrigerator to help himself to another beer. Bill bit his bottom lip as if he was gonna say something, but he thought better of it and followed Henry out into the living room.

Tension bled out of the kitchen when the two men left. "Sorry 'bout that," Julie said softly.

"No reason for you to apologize," Franklin told her. "You want me to kick them out now?"

"No," Julie said. "But it might be a really early night."

"Fine by me," Franklin assured her, kissing her again on the cheek just 'cause he could.

Then he helped himself to a beer and walked out into the living room to join the other men. He settled himself in one of the folding chairs, as Henry had sprawled out across the entire love seat, and Bill had taken the over stuffed chair that sat in front of the front door. There was also a rocker in the corner, but that was for Julie and the baby.

Franklin sat and quietly sipped his beer, breathing in the room. He'd never seen the need to fill the air with useless chatter.

"So how's the vegetable stand going?" Bill asked. It was obvious that he was trying to play nice. At least nicer than Henry.

What was going on with him?

"It's doing well," Franklin said. "We're holding a pumpkin carving contest," he added.

"How does that work?" Bill asked, sounding genuinely interested. Bill didn't own the car repair shop where he worked, though he could have. He'd made the decision long ago that he weren't interested in the paperwork involved, instead just wanting to work on cars. Luckily, he'd found an owner who would, to quote him, "leave him the hell alone" and let him work his magic.

However, Bill was interested in business, how it ran, how to grow it. He and Franklin had been using that as common ground since Bill had no interest in plants or crops, and Franklin had little interest in cars.

Franklin laid out the details, about the stickers they'd had made special for the pumpkins they was selling, getting people to post pictures of their carvings or bring them to the stall. Karl had an Instagram account where he'd been putting all the photos. They'd make their decision at the end of the month and choose a winner.

"You might, some year, think about renting a tent and holding the carving contest on site," Bill suggested. "Bring in a lot of people to just watch kids carving, and adults, too."

"We've considered that," Franklin said. "It would be easier if we could guarantee the weather, though. Since we'd be outside, if it were pouring rain, we'd have to maybe postpone."

"True enough," Bill said. "Well, maybe a combination of both."

Franklin nodded. "If it's popular enough this year, that would be a good way to expand it."

"You'd have to get permits," Henry chimed in.

"We'd certainly do that," Franklin agreed. Then, because he was feeling more mellow, Franklin asked Henry, "And how's the policing going?"

Franklin was sure sorry he asked as Henry went into a rant about the lousy teenagers in this county and the next, how they was making his life hell. Between the legalized marijuana, the graffiti, and the runaways, it was getting harder and harder to keep up.

"What runaways?" Franklin asked when he could get a word in edgewise.

"Kids," Henry said. He looked as though he'd like to spit, but remembered at the last minute just where he was. "They're all running away now. Younger and younger."

"You sure they're runaways? And not being kidnapped or something?" Franklin asked. "We got that one boy, Hollis Chambers, here."

"How'd you hear about Hollis?" Henry asked, shooting a hard look at Franklin.

"Sheriff come by the stand with fliers, asking us to display a few," Franklin said casually.

"He's not the only kid," Henry said. "But because his parents are so rich, they've been bothering us every day for updates. They make a habit of going from one office to the next, and carrying their posse of reports with them."

"They're parents," Franklin pointed out. "They're worried about their son. I would be too."

Bill had to agree, but Henry weren't done yet. "You know what I think? That boy run off with his older brother to Louisville. Kids don't want to stay down here on the farm, in the country anymore."

"Are you sure?" Franklin had to ask.

"Hell, yes!" Henry said. "His big brother just came to pick him up, scooped him out of the street. Happens that way sometimes."

"And where's the big brother now?" Bill asked.

"Living with his girlfriend. They don't have a permanent residence." Henry shook his head. "Harder than hell to track people like that. And you can't believe them. People like that lie as easily as they breathe."

"What if Hollis wasn't picked up by his brother? But by someone else?" Franklin asked quietly.

"Then why haven't they asked for any ransom? The Chambers can afford it," Henry said. "I think they're offering too much already. You wouldn't believe the number of crank calls we been getting in. Hell, half of them seem to think the boy's in the next state over."

"What are the chances that the boy's still alive?" Bill asked. "I mean, isn't it some sort of statistic that the longer a child is missing, the less likely he'll be found alive?"

Henry gave an ugly laugh. It sent chills up Franklin's spine. It was the laugh of someone who'd just given up and didn't care about much of anything anymore.

They was definitely gonna have an early night tonight.

"Don't you see? It don't really matter. The boy's already done all the damage he can, by encouraging other boys to just take off," Henry explained.

"And what if he didn't take off?" Franklin said. "What if you got some kind of monster on your hands who's taking white boys?"

Henry shot Franklin a hard look. "You know something?"

"No," Franklin lied, sitting back and shaking his head.

"You know something about the missing boys," Henry insisted.

"I do not," Franklin said. "I just said that you should consider the possibility."

Henry narrowed his eyes at Franklin but didn't say another word.

"Dinner's ready," Julie announced.

Franklin sprang up from his chair to go help her serve. But

as soon as dinner was finished, so was he. The guests would be politely asked to leave so Julie could get her much needed sleep.

Franklin wasn't about to put up with any more antics from anyone.

~

LATER THAT NIGHT, FRANKLIN SAT ON THE LOVESEAT WITH Julie curled up in his lap. It weren't as comfortable for either of them as it had once been—Julie had a difficult time finding a way to lay against him, and Franklin found his arms and legs going to sleep from the extra weight.

He wasn't about to complain none. Having Julie in his arms was the highlight of his day.

The other highlights, like the intimacy they shared, would come back after the babe had started sleeping through the night. Or at least that was what Julie assured him.

"Want to tell me what happened?" Franklin asked Julie after they'd settled in, enjoying the quiet. The living room still smelled of new plastic baby toys, but underlaying it was the scent of their good food. The sour smell that Henry had brought with him had finally vanished.

They kept the lights off, just sitting in the dark. The bedroom light was on, the dim one next to the bed, taking all the edges off.

"Uncle Henry just makes me so mad sometimes," Julie said with a sigh. "I don't think he means any harm. But he thinks he knows it all when it comes to parents and kids."

"Has he ever had any?" Franklin asked. He'd thought that Henry may have inherited kids, but he'd never had any of his own.

"Nope," Julie said. She settled in closer, pushing herself

against Franklin's strong shoulders. He held her tighter, kissing her forehead, willing to wait and hear her out.

"He wants to blame the parents. Or the kids. Like you brought up, he won't even consider that someone out there is preying on them." She shivered. "And I bet, even if someone is caught, Uncle Henry would still blame the kids for being caught."

"That's not right," Franklin said. He sighed himself and hugged Julie again for a moment.

"Out with it," Julie said. "I can tell that something's bothering you, and it wasn't just dinner. You been like this for a couple days now."

Franklin nodded, feeling Julie's soft hair slide against his cheek. "Hollis is dead," he said softly.

Julie pulled Franklin in closer. "I suspected as such, that he was the ghost you were seeing."

"It ain't right," Franklin said. He told her about the boy and his worries, since Hollis wore shorts and not a good suit, since his light seemed so worn down. "And now there's a second boy. Andrew."

Julie gave a quiet gasp. "There's been an announcement on the radio about him."

"And…there's something else." Franklin shook his head. "I don't want to tell you about it. But I promised you that I'd trust you with everything."

"I can help you carry the burden," Julie told him softly. "I can't carry it for you. I do believe though, that sharing it will help."

"I know," Franklin said. "It's just hard. I ain't never had someone I could talk to before. Not like this. Not even with Mama."

"So tell me," Julie said. "I promise I won't tell no one else. Not even your mama."

Franklin grinned. "I appreciate that," he told her solemnly. Then he told her about the ice cream truck and Mr. Orville.

"I need to follow him some night," Franklin said. "That's the only way I can think of to find him. Darryl can't track him —says cars are unnatural and don't leave enough of a trail."

"Can't you tell the police?" Julie asked.

Franklin snorted. "Not like they'd believe me. I don't have a lick of evidence. Now, I know you don't like to think like this. But what would a white sheriff do to a black man who came in and started talking about dead white boys?"

"He'd be a fool and arrest the black man," Julie said. "You're right, I don't like to think about that sort of thing. I'd want to believe the white sheriff would do the right thing. I also know the truth. You go in and start talking about dead white boys, and you're gonna have to watch your own baby grow up from behind bars."

"Yup," Franklin said. "And I don't know what's making him do it, either. Is he being influenced by some creature? Is there a demon out there directing him? Or is he just evil?"

"I'm sorry," Julie said, shaking her head against his chest. "I'm so sorry."

Franklin felt the splash of the first few tears against his shirt. "What you sorry about?" he asked, holding her tight. "You don't got nothing to be sorry about."

"It's just me," Julie said after a moment, sniffing mightily. "Stupid pregnancy hormones. But I was just thinking about how sad you'd be if something happened to our baby."

"I know," Franklin said. He knew he could tear up at the thought as well. "But we're gonna do our best. Love them every day. Tell 'em we're proud of him or her."

"Or both of them. All of them," Julie said.

"Exactly," Franklin said. He was planning on loving them as much as he loved Julie. And Mama. And popping corn. He had enough love for all that, and more.

"So what are you going to do?" Julie asked after a few moments of more cuddling, her sniffles gradually dying away.

"I don't know," Franklin said. "We're talking with Tommy later this week. Maybe he can help me see the future and tell me what I'm supposed to do."

CHAPTER 8

"HELLO?" FRANKLIN SAID AS THEY WALKED INTO DARRYL'S house on Friday night, ready to have dinner with the family. "Anybody here?"

Georgia came out of the kitchen into the front hallway. "Good to see you both!" she said as she took the large bowl of salad from Franklin's hands. She was still in her work clothes, a nice navy blue skirt and pale pink shirt, appropriate for the insurance agency she worked in. "Good lord," she announced looking at Julie. "You look about ready to burst."

"Feel that way," Julie said. "I know the baby's not due for a few weeks. But I think it wants to be born tomorrow, if it had its way." She'd been complaining about how even her comfy gray pants, the kind that was soft like sweat pants, were getting too tight.

"Why didn't you bother learning the sex of the baby?" Georgia asked as she took Julie's coat and hung it in the closet. "I would think you'd want to know."

Julie shrugged. "Wanted it to be a surprise, I guess. Though more than one of the nurses at the hospital have told me that they think it's a girl."

"Why's that?" Georgia asked.

"I got clear skin," Julie said. "Boy baby makes a mama break out because of all the conflicting hormones. Girl baby makes mama's skin look radiant."

"You'd look radiant anyway, my darling," Franklin said as he took Julie's hand.

Before Franklin could lead Julie out to the couch and insist that she put her feet up, Tommy came upstairs from the basement. "Uncle Franklin! Uncle Franklin! You gotta come see the cool space Pa built for me." He was wearing a long-sleeved T-shirt, red with a burst of white graffiti across the chest, and jeans, looking more like a young man every day.

"She'll be all right," Georgia said, directing Franklin toward the door to the downstairs. "I'll make sure that she sits down right now, with her feet up."

"Thank you," Franklin said. Just as he wanted to be able to take care of their child all the time, he wanted to do the same with Julie as well.

Franklin followed Tommy down the stairs into the damp basement. It were only half built out. The walls were all finished but they'd just had a single coat of white paint on them. The laundry room was to the left of the stairs, underneath the dining room. To the right stood the extra freezer and shelves for storage.

"This way," Tommy said. He walked to his right, then kept going.

Darryl had closed off an area underneath the stairs. The walls were made of storage boxes. A towel hung over the doorway. It was barely bigger than a closet and smelled of the basement, dank and wet, with the chemical sweetness of laundry detergent overlaying it. The chill in the place washed over Franklin, like a gaggle of ghosts was nesting here.

However, it was Tommy's space. It had big "Stay out!" signs taped to the boxes and pinned to the towel, done in red magic marker, with skulls and crossbones.

"See? And it has a desk and a chair and enough light and everything!" Tommy gushed on.

"It's a nice place," Franklin declared, though he didn't like it much. He didn't care for being underground like this. He wanted to be outside, out in the open, in his fields. It was too cold and damp down here. He looked around again, goosebumps rising across his neck. But he didn't see no ghosts.

"And see?" Tommy said, sitting down at the little desk. It was made out of half a door laying across the tops of milk cartons. "I got space here for doing my readings. Ma found me some notebooks when I asked her to. And I got a second chair here and everything!"

Franklin obliged his nephew by sitting down on the little stool. The top rotated on its own.

"You planning on bringing strangers down here?" Franklin asked, pointing at the half-drawn sign on Tommy's desk, offering tarot readings.

Tommy shrugged. "I don't know about here. This is for the winter fair at school. We're supposed to come up with something that we can make money at, for charity. Vashmi, the Indian guy, is going to make people their own individual curry blends. Ilsa is planning on teaching how to crochet these tiny fuzzy mice. I figured I could do readings."

"Makes sense," Franklin said. "That's a lot of work, though."

"Yeah, but it would be fun," Tommy insisted. "Don't think most of them would mean anything. Just be making stuff up."

"Not all the time," Franklin pointed out.

"No, the cards would be talking to me some of the time," Tommy admitted.

"You gonna let people know you're different if you do that," Franklin felt obliged to point out.

Tommy snorted. "Half the class already calls me that 'cause of you, Uncle Franklin."

"What do you mean?" Franklin asked. He'd know that half the town believed that he talked with ghosts because of Mama. It had been years since those stories had been passed around. He'd hoped that some of the gossip would have died down by now.

"Kids know you're different," Tommy said with a shrug. "It's why they drag their parents to the fruit and vegetable stand. Some of 'em swear it's haunted."

"The ghosts don't bother the stand much," Franklin said. Mostly they stayed at the farm. A few did follow him to work, but it didn't happen often.

"What about last month? When that whole stack of potatoes just fell over?" Tommy asked. "Couple of kids got that recorded on their cell phones. Pile was just fine one moment, then tumbling over the next."

"All right, so maybe there was that one ghost," Franklin admitted. Been an angry young man who'd wanted Franklin to take him to the VFW lodge the next town over. Franklin hadn't had time before work, but the ghost hadn't wanted to wait.

Tommy raised both his eyebrows and looked like he didn't believe his uncle.

"There have been a few ghosts at the stand," Franklin grumbled. "Not too many though. Maybe every other month."

"Just enough to keep things interesting," Tommy said.

Franklin didn't know about *interesting*, though he didn't contradict Tommy.

"So you told your parents yet?" Franklin asked.

"Boys! Dinner!" Georgia called down the stairs.

Franklin stood up, but he didn't go anywhere. Not until he heard Tommy's answer.

"They probably already know," Tommy said. Then he sighed and shook his head. "No, they don't. But I'm aiming to tell them tonight, after dinner."

"That's good," Franklin said, patting Tommy on the shoulder. "It's gonna be all right."

Tommy shot Franklin a questioning look at that, opened his mouth, then shut it again.

"Dinner! Now!" Georgia said firmly.

"Yes, ma'am!" Franklin called, heading out of the tiny space and up the stairs.

He weren't sure what Tommy still had to say to his uncle. He suspected he'd hear about it later, though.

Darryl, Georgia, and Julie all sat together on the long black couch, while Franklin sat to one side. Joanne was in her room doing homework, while Pete had already gone to bed. Darryl had changed out of his work uniform into jeans and a white T-shirt, though he weren't as greasy as usual. He'd broken his arm a few years back and had been switched to inventory. Turned out he had a pretty good head for keeping track of all the parts they needed. Plus, for him, it was its own form of hunting, tracking down specialty parts when they got fancy cars.

Tommy stood in front of them, looking like he was facing a firing squad.

Franklin wanted to assure the boy that he'd be okay. He just needed to keep breathing. But Tommy—no, Tom, the young man—had to do this on his own.

"Ma, Pa, I got something to tell you," Tom said. He stood up taller and put his hands behind his back.

"Now, first off, I want to tell you that I'm not gay," he said. He glared at Darryl. "I'm really not. All those hints you been leaving have just been embarrassing."

Darryl shrugged and didn't seem embarrassed at all. "We just wanted you to know that we supported you, son."

"Didn't think you even knew what a rainbow flag was," Tom admitted. "But I didn't need one planted in the middle of my bed."

Franklin snorted. Darryl wasn't about to do anything in half measures.

"Then what is going on?" Georgia asked quietly. "You can tell us."

Tom sighed, looked at his shoes, then looked up again. "I can do things. Different things. Like Uncle Franklin."

"You can see ghosts?" Darryl asked. He seemed more curious than mad. Would that come later?

"No," Tom said. "I can sometimes predict the future." He pulled out the deck of tarot cards from one of the pockets of his jeans. "I use these. There's stories in the cards. I can see 'em. Hear 'em."

"Any cards?" Georgia asked.

Tom nodded and said, "I think so. It's why I had that one deck hidden outside. The cards were talking to me, all the time. I had to get them out of the house."

"So what happened that night?" Darryl asked. "Did you go to visit them or something?"

"Couldn't sleep. Felt like the cards were laying on the bed right next to my pillow, whispering to me," Tom admitted. "I had to go out and see them. They calmed down after I shuffled them a few times. Then I went back into the house."

"How long do you think you were in the backyard?" Franklin asked.

"Couple minutes," Tom said, shrugging.

"You were gone for a lot longer than that," Darryl stated. "And I couldn't find you."

"I didn't see you come into the back," Tom said. "I could only see the cards."

Darryl and Franklin shared a look. Both of them were confused. How had Tommy just disappeared that way? Was it because he was so focused on the cards? Had they hid him?

"Why don't you show us what you can do?" Franklin suggested.

"Okay," Tom said. He easily folded himself and sat down on the floor, on the far side of the coffee table. He pulled the tarot cards out of the box and shuffled them easily.

Darryl and Georgia glanced at each other when they noticed how their boy changed once he started working with the deck. Franklin hoped they saw how Tommy was becoming Tom, right before their eyes.

"I'll do you, Pa," Tom said after he'd shuffled for a bit. He handed the deck to Darryl. "Cut the cards."

Darryl just reached out and tapped the top of the deck.

Tom nodded. He flipped over the first card. "This is your past." It showed a blond man hanging upside down from a tree. The card was colorful, and the man on the card looked at peace. "This is a card of learning, of focus, and sacrifice," Tom explained. "You've been spending your time doing different things, learning a new way of living."

Franklin wasn't sure if the cards were talking to Tom or not, as the first card seemed kind of obvious to him.

"This is the present," Tom said, flipping over the next card. "Eight of staves."

Eight pieces of wood looked like they was flying through the air. The staves was still alive, with green twigs growing on them. The sky behind them was blue, and a river flowed nearby.

"More searching," Tom said firmly. "You're still looking for something. I wouldn't say hunting, not yet. You haven't flushed your prey yet. But you're in motion, ready to fly."

Franklin blinked, surprised. What was Darryl supposed to be moving toward? That didn't make a lot of sense.

"And this is the future," Tom said. It was a young man charging ahead on a horse, with his sword drawn. "Knight of swords," he continued. "Charging ahead without a lot of thought about the consequences, sure he's right. Notice the clouds in the background," he added. "The knight is racing ahead, into the storm."

Tom shook his head after a moment. "This is where it gets confusing for me," he admitted. "Past and present are pretty clear. The future, though. Is it a good thing you're charging ahead? Am I supposed to encourage you to do it? Warn you away? I just don't know."

"That's okay," Darryl said. "Where did you get these cards from?"

"They were my mama's," Franklin said. "I don't know about the other deck, but it might have been hers, too."

"Your ma used to tell fortunes at the hair salon, didn't she?" Georgia said slowly. "I remember that now."

Franklin nodded. "She always said it was just for fun. But I think she saw the true future a couple of times."

"I don't know what exactly I'm seeing," Tom said. "Sometimes it's just for fun. Other times, it isn't." He looked solemn as he picked up the cards and put them away. "But that's why I need my space. Downstairs. So I can sit with the cards and listen to their stories. And the notebooks," he added. "So I can write down what I see sometimes."

Darryl and Georgia looked blankly at each other. This hadn't been what they'd been expecting to hear.

"You're still going to have to do the dishes, clean your room, help with your brother and sister," Darryl added after a bit. "I don't care if the cards is talking to you right then. You're expected to help out around the house, first."

"Yes, sir," Tommy said. He gave a big grin. "How'd you know I was thinking about using them to get out of my chores?"

Georgia rolled her eyes. "Because you're *his* son," she said.

Both Franklin and Julie grinned at Darryl's faked outrage.

"Now, since I'm assuming that this came from *your* side of the family," Georgia continued, turning her sharp gaze on Franklin, "do you think that there may be other surprises as well?"

"What do you mean?" Franklin asked.

"Pete? Joanne? They got any powers?" Georgia asked.

"I got no idea," Franklin said. "But Tommy—Tom—is about the right age. I started seeing ghosts when I was a little younger than him."

"Preacher Sinclair isn't gonna like it," Georgia said. "But then again, it might not be any of his business. Am I right?" she asked, taking a moment to look at all the adults in the room.

"That's right," Franklin said. "He already knows about me, though I think half the time he don't even believe it. But he never has to know about anyone else."

"Good," Georgia said. She speared Tommy with a look. "I wouldn't tell your other cousins just yet either."

Tom nodded. "I haven't told Pete or Joanne either."

"You might have to tell them sooner rather than later," Georgia admitted. "They're already asking about the room in the basement."

"Do they want their own space, too?" Franklin asked, curious.

"Only cause Tommy has one," Darryl said. "Maybe we'll have to think about getting spaces for them when they're older."

Georgia shrugged. "They've never been asking for one before. Not like Tommy did. He's always wanted his own space, ever since he was a young boy."

Tommy nodded. "Don't know why. Just…needed it."

"It's why I go hunting," Darryl said. "That's my space and time."

Was Darryl ever gonna admit that he had some sort of gift too? That he was that good at hunting? Darryl glanced over at Georgia, who shook her head.

Maybe not yet. Was it because Tommy weren't ready? Or Darryl?

"I'm proud of you," Franklin told Tommy as they was getting ready to go. "That couldn't have been easy."

"You made it easier, Uncle Franklin," Tommy said. "You never let my pa run all over you. Most of the time."

"I don't much stand with being bullied," Franklin admitted. "Not by him, or the sheriff, or nobody."

Tommy nodded thoughtfully. "The cards…they aren't trying to be bullies. They just want to be heard. Like the ghosts."

"Exactly," Franklin said. "And I need to do my duty to the ghosts."

"I'll try to do my duty as well," Tommy said seriously. "Did it ever scare you?"

"All the damned time," Franklin said. "But that's what being brave's for. Not 'cause it's easy. But because it's right."

"Thanks, Uncle Franklin," Tommy said. He held out his hand to shake like a man. "I'll let you know how it goes." Then he went to his bedroom.

"What was that all about?" Julie asked as they got into the car.

"I'm not quite sure," Franklin said. "I think there's something else going on with that boy."

"It'll be all right," Julie assured him.

Franklin got a chill again, like a ghost was passing nearby.

Would it be all right? He felt doubt for the first time.

FRANKLIN AND KARL WERE JUST FINISHING UP THE morning shift when Sheriff Thompson came driving up in his brown Crown Vic. The sheriff had brought a deputy with him, one who Franklin didn't recognize. While the sheriff wore a dark brown jacket over his tan uniform, the deputy was in solid black jacket, like it was cut out of a starless night.

The only soft thing about Sheriff Thompson was his long brown mustache. The new deputy didn't have anything soft about him at all. His brown eyes was harder than coconut shells, frown lines marked either side of his thin lips, and his sharp nose looked like it was excellent for getting into other people's business.

"Franklin Kanly?" Sheriff Thompson said as he got closer to the stand.

"That's me, sheriff," Franklin said. This weren't no social call, not with the sheriff being all formal and such. "Whatcha need?"

"Can you step outside the stand?" the deputy asked. His eyes blazed at Franklin.

"All right," Franklin said. He didn't want this deputy messing with their stand. He looked all tense and wired up, like he was a bomb set to go off.

"Call Julie," Franklin told Karl as he passed, heading out the side. Then he walked slowly up to the sheriff, keeping his hands in plain view. "What's this about?"

"Franklin Kanly, we need to bring you in for questioning regarding the disappearance of Hollis Chambers," Sheriff Thompson said formally. He kept his back stiff and his face looked blank.

"I didn't kill that boy, sheriff, and you know it," Franklin said stubbornly.

The sheriff gave a deep sigh. "I figured that," he said, shooting his deputy a hard look. "But we got a strongly worded request from Edmonds county, next door, that we take a good long look at you."

"What?" Franklin asked, confused. "Why would they have anything to do with me?" He didn't know anyone from the next county over, did he?

"Oh," Franklin said after a moment. "Henry Horton works over there, don't he? In that sheriff's office?"

The new deputy didn't answer. But Franklin had what he needed.

"I'll come talk with you gentlemen," Franklin said after a moment. "But I ain't under arrest, and I can leave at any time," he added, asking for clarification.

"That's right," Sheriff Thompson said.

The deputy just looked disgusted, as if he hadn't wanted Franklin to know.

"I'll be back after lunch," Franklin told Karl as he headed for the police car. "Don't worry about calling Julie until then."

He was gonna cooperate, despite how he knew Darryl would cus him out and call him all kinds of fool for even talking to the police.

But he was also determined that they wasn't gonna push him too far or he'd just walk out of there.

CHAPTER 9

FRANKLIN SAT IN A TINY INTERVIEW ROOM. THERE WAS room for a desk, two chairs on one side, and a single chair on the other. He figured it was a one-way mirror in front of him, and that there was officers staring at him on the other. It smelled like bleach and filtered air, nothing natural in here.

They'd at least offered him some coffee, not that he drank the stuff. Then they let him sit.

He tried not to be bothered by it. He'd seen too many TV shows where the cops let someone stew, hoping to sweat them and make them make a mistake.

Franklin weren't guilty, had nothing to worry about. Except getting back to the stand before Karl called Julie. He didn't want to worry her none. She'd been less tired that morning, had a happy smile for him when she woke up. The baby had been really active too, kicking her sides, like he or she was anxious to get out now.

The cops hadn't taken away his cell phone or anything, though there weren't any reception here. So Franklin read through all the text messages he'd received from Julie, feeling warm and loved all over again.

When it had been just about an hour, Franklin stood up, ready to walk out of there.

Right then, Sheriff Thompson and the deputy came waltzing in. Franklin sat back down and nodded to them. They'd probably been waiting for him to run out of patience.

"So what can you tell us about Hollis Chambers?" Sheriff Thompson said.

"He disappeared more than a week ago," Franklin said. "Henry Horton seems to think Hollis ran off to be with his big brother in the city."

"What do you think happened?" the deputy asked.

Franklin bit his lip, considering. Was they not gonna do good cop/bad cop? He'd kinda been looking forward to seeing that in person.

"I think he was taken," Franklin admitted. "Off Ellis Street. Right where he dropped his bike." He weren't gonna say nothing more.

"You sure he dropped his bike there?" Sheriff Thompson asked. "We have reports of him riding up Main street after that."

"That's what the papers said," he replied. "That he dropped his bike like a careless boy on Ellis."

He knew what had happened. He'd seen it with the other two boys and the ice cream truck.

"Why would he do that?" the deputy asked.

"Maybe he saw someone he knew," Franklin said. "No struggle, right?"

"Do you know the boy?" the sheriff asked.

"No, sir. I never laid eyes on him," Franklin said. He bit his tongue so he wouldn't add anything more, like that he'd never seen the boy alive. Dead, sure, plenty of him, except for the last few nights.

"You been seeing his ghost?" the sheriff asked.

Franklin blinked, surprised. "Now, why would you think I could do something like that?" he asked. Darryl would have been proud of how well he'd been lying.

"Everyone's heard the reports," the deputy said. "They all know you're crazy."

Franklin just shrugged. He weren't about to argue with this stranger.

"I think you know more about this boy than you want to admit," Sheriff Thompson said with a sigh.

Damn. Maybe Franklin weren't that good at lying to the cops.

"Particularly since you've been up to Ellis Street, just the other day," the deputy said. "Talking to a couple of boys there. Spooked them."

Franklin blinked. He'd just been trying to be friendly.

"I know, you were curious about where the Hollis boy had been taken," Sheriff Thompson said.

"That's right," Franklin admitted. "I was curious."

"Or you was revisiting the scene of the crime," the deputy added. He had a smug smile on his face, as if he'd just trapped Franklin.

Damn it! Franklin saw his mistake now. He shouldn't have admitted to being up there.

Then again, he had told those two white boys his name.

"I was just curious," Franklin told them again. "Don't see no harm in that."

"Except that you know more about Hollis than you're telling us," the sheriff said. "You've been seeing his ghost."

Franklin snorted. "You been watching too much TV to

believe I can actually talk to ghosts." He didn't, not really. He did a lot more listening than talking.

Not that Franklin thought the sheriff would actually believe him if he admitted to it.

The sheriff and the deputy glanced at each other, before the sheriff nodded. He stood up slowly. "Franklin Kanly, we're arresting you for the murder of Hollis Chambers."

"You're what?" Franklin asked, confused. "You know I didn't kill him," Franklin protested as he stood up.

"You have the right to an attorney," the sheriff continued.

"Why you doing this?" Franklin asked the deputy.

He shrugged. "Couldn't talk him into putting a psych hold on you. Then we could have nabbed you for thirty days."

Franklin shivered at the cold hard look the deputy gave him.

The sheriff droned on about how an attorney would be provided to Franklin, asking if he understood the rights being read to him.

"I understand," Franklin said.

He weren't guilty. The sheriff knew that.

But the sheriff was a fool if he thought that throwing Franklin in jail overnight was gonna get him to change his mind about anything.

FRANKLIN SPENT THE DAY IN THE HOLDING CELL LOCATED in the police station, not in the county jail or in prison. The cops hadn't charged him yet, just arrested him on suspicion of murder.

They didn't have any proof. Franklin wasn't about to say anything to the sheriff either, though he thought of the one question he really wanted to know: had Hollis been taken on a sunny day? He figured Mr. Orville and the ice cream truck only came around when it was nice.

But he didn't see how he could even ask that without making the sheriff more suspicious.

It weren't the first time Franklin had spent time in the local holding cell. Located at the back of the regular police station on Main Street, he got to watch the cops do their job all day. It seemed pretty ordinary, with paperwork and cracking jokes.

He didn't know what to do with himself. The bench he sat on was big enough that he could lay down, but he didn't feel much like sleeping. The air in here was too thin, not fresh enough to breathe. He suspected that if he'd ever been thrown in a real jail, he'd likely go crazy. He couldn't think of being anywhere worse, where there weren't no fresh air or light.

Julie came to see him when her shift was over. They held hands through the bars. Franklin didn't like seeing the worry in her eyes, or how she looked as though she'd been crying.

"It's all right," Franklin told her. "They ain't charged me with nothing. They's just trying to see if they can get me to blink."

It put his back up, just how much the sheriff seemed to be trying to bully Franklin. And Franklin didn't stand for no bullying, not from the sheriff or no one.

"I know," Julie said. She sniffed, as if the tears was about to start again. "I just...I get worried. I don't want your baby to only know you through bars."

"Won't happen," Franklin said. "I didn't do it."

"I know, I know," Julie said. "They might still try something stupid."

Franklin shook his head. "They's just holding me," he told her again.

Julie nodded. "I expect you home tomorrow night," she told him firmly. "And every night."

"Yes, ma'am," Franklin said, though he felt it were a little unfair. It hadn't been his idea to stay here for the evening.

After Julie left, Franklin tried to settle himself down and sleep some. But he kept hearing strange noises, like ghosts who couldn't make up their mind whether to visit or not.

Franklin knew he had to continue doing his duty. Not just 'cause Mama had beat it into him, but because it were the right thing to do.

Not telling the sheriff that Hollis Chambers were dead was also the right thing to do. If Franklin wanted to be able to help the boy, he needed to be on the other side of these prison bars.

However, things got a bit more murky after that. How could Franklin tell the cops about the ice cream truck? Sheriff Thompson wouldn't believe Franklin that a ghost had told him. He'd think there was something else going on, and maybe arrest Franklin again. Maybe do—what had the deputy called it? A psych hold?

Franklin couldn't be in a jail for thirty days. That would make him crazy.

But he also knew that Darryl was right. Franklin couldn't say nothing to no one about the boys and his suspicions.

Even if that meant more jail time.

Sheriff Thompson showed up at the holding cell bright and early in the morning, before they'd even brought Franklin his breakfast.

"Seems your free to go," the sheriff said as he opened the cell.

The sheriff didn't look happy about it. He had the start of dark circles under his eyes, as if his own ghosts had been keeping him up all night.

"What's this about, Sheriff?" Franklin asked, though he was glad he was getting out early.

"Got word from higher up to let you go free. Right now, before I'd even finished my own damned coffee," Sheriff Thompson replied. "Somebody put the fear of God into the mayor on your behalf. I'd be sure to thank him later."

"Who did that?" Franklin asked. He couldn't have been more surprised. He didn't know nobody important. Who'd gone and bent the ear of the mayor?

Sheriff Thompson just shrugged.

Franklin took a deep breath as he walked out of the police center. He didn't think no air had ever smelled as good. While he had vowed to never take Julie for granted, he was suspecting that maybe he needed to treasure his freedom the same way.

A light drizzle filled the morning air. Franklin shivered despite the heavy canvas jacket he was wearing. He started walking toward the fruit and vegetable stand. It would take him a while to get there, but he'd probably get there sooner rather than waiting on Karl to take a break.

Franklin's stomach rumbled with hunger. He wasn't gonna stop anywhere, though. He'd just have one of those power bars that Karl kept at the back of the stand, even though Franklin thought they was overly sweet and had a nasty powdery taste to them.

As Franklin was taking his phone out of his pocket so he could call Julie and let her know he was out of jail, it rang. He nearly dropped it he was so startled.

Then he saw who was calling.

"Morning, Ray," Franklin said. "Do I have you to thank for my freedom this lovely morning?"

"They never would have charged you," Ray Sorrel on the other end of the line told him. "They were just trying to hold you to see if you would talk."

"There weren't nothing I could have told them," Franklin said as he kept walking down the sidewalk. "Except that the boy's already dead."

Ray sighed. "That's a sad thing."

"It is," Franklin agreed. "Still, thank you for getting me out of jail quicker. You didn't have to do that."

"I know," Ray said. "Just seemed like the right thing to do."

"How'd you hear about me being arrested in the first place?" Franklin asked. Ray lived down in Florida. Franklin would have known if Ray had come up to Kentucky.

Then he grinned. Of course, that was why Sheriff Thompson had sprung him so early. Because Ray had been haranguing the mayor ever since dawn.

"I got my ears open for you," Ray admitted. "Anytime anything comes up in police headquarters regarding you or your family, I get notified."

Franklin gave a low whistle. "You don't have to do that," Franklin said. "We're gonna be all right." How did Ray do that? Did he have a paid informant in police headquarters? Franklin wasn't sure how he felt about that.

"I know," Ray said. "Just consider me your guardian angel at large."

"Thank you," Franklin said.

"How's that beautiful bride of yours?" Ray asked.

"I don't know how she does it, but she gets prettier every day," Franklin said.

"I know just how you feel," Ray said. "I felt the same way about Adrianna."

"How are you doing?" Franklin asked after a moment of shared sadness passed between them. Adrianna had been special, a charming white woman who could see lines of power in the land. After the creature had killed her, Franklin had made sure to talk with Ray every week, and him and Julie had dinner with Ray at least once a month, sometimes more.

According to Ray, they'd helped him stay sane after his wife's death.

Even after Ray had moved down to Florida, Franklin had stubbornly called Ray once a week, making sure that he was doing okay.

"I love the sunshine down here," Ray admitted. "And nothing beats living on the ocean."

Ray had sent Franklin some pictures taken from his front deck. White sand, dark gray waters, and blue sky had filled the frame.

Franklin supposed there were a kind of peace watching the waves that way. It just weren't for him.

"I'm glad you found your place," Franklin said. That was what mattered, though sometimes he missed seeing Ray. Ray had spent most of his life out in Hollywood, and knew all kinds of things about movies and the people making them.

"I'm still planning on coming up for my godchild's christening," Ray said.

Franklin grinned. "It'll be good to see you," he said. "Julie's not due for a couple of weeks, but she keeps saying that the baby wants to be born quicker."

It had made sense to them to make Ray the godparent of their child. As Ray had said, he was kind of like their guardian angel.

Ray chuckled. "Or she's just tired of being pregnant." He paused, then added, "You know what I've heard about getting a baby to come sooner?"

"What's that?"

"Go take her to have a pedicure. Baby will see those pretty toes and want to have a closer look," Ray explained.

Franklin snorted. He didn't think that any baby of his would be drawn to pretty toes, but there was an awful lot he didn't know about birth and babies.

"I'll tell Julie about what you said," Franklin told Ray.

"All right. You have a good day," Ray said.

"You, too," Franklin replied. "And thank you again."

"Gotta take care of my family," Ray said as he hung up.

Was Ray family? Franklin supposed that was true. Franklin had done his best to take care of Ray after Adrianna had died, him and Julie kind of adopting him, then asking him to be the godparent for their first born.

It had just been the right thing to do, to help Ray get through his grief. Though Franklin doubted Ray would ever "get over" Adrianna. You just didn't do that.

He called Julie next, reassuring her that he was fine, letting her know what Ray did.

He knew who his next call was gonna have to be.

Darryl.

They had to find that ice cream man. Mr. Orville. And put a stop to him breaking up families for good.

FRANKLIN SPENT THE DAY YAWNING WHILE WORKING AT the fruit and vegetable stand. As it was Saturday and their busiest day, Karl made Franklin stand at the back and restock.

They had two teenagers helping deal with customers, and more importantly, count change as Franklin were just too tired to keep the numbers right.

He just hadn't slept in that holding cell, too worried about his future, his baby's future, his family's future. He didn't know what he was gonna do once he and Darryl found Mr. Orville. Franklin weren't about to shoot him or something.

How could they catch this Mr. Orville in the act? Fall was taking a good hold, the days never really warming up no matter how sunny it was. He couldn't be driving his ice cream truck around all day. Besides, his other job would be taking up most of his time now, driving a school bus.

Franklin didn't have skills to do something crazy like break into the police database and look up Mr. Orville's driver's license. He didn't know anyone who did, and he weren't about to ask Ray for help. Ray and him were out of favors for one another. Anything Ray did for Franklin or his family was just that—for family.

And what would Franklin do when he found Mr. Orville? Tell him to stop killing boys? What good would that do? While Franklin could shoot, he weren't about to take no gun with him. That was a sure way to get himself thrown in jail. While Franklin was strong, he wasn't about to kill a man.

All he could do would be to tell Mr. Orville no. He couldn't keep doing this.

That wouldn't be enough, however.

Julie came to pick Franklin up at the end of the day. Though Franklin didn't tend to kiss Julie in public, and maybe they'd hold hands now and again, particularly when they went to see the movies or something, he couldn't help himself when she came up to the stand, walking in back. Franklin just wrapped his arms around her, holding her tightly.

Particularly since he'd been contemplating his future all day long.

Franklin held on, just for a bit. He needed her strength and warmth. She still had that good womanly smell that was as much home as the farm, now. Her belly stuck out proudly.

Though if Franklin were any judge, he'd say that she was carrying different now. Used to be the baby sat up higher. Seemed to him that most of Julie's weight had dropped some, lower in her belly.

"Hi, darling," Franklin said, kissing her lightly on the lips, extra thrilled today that he could do that.

"Hi," Julie said, giving him a tired smile. "You look as exhausted as I feel."

"Early bed for both of us," Franklin told her seriously.

Tomorrow, well, tomorrow he'd have to go hunting with Darryl. After church, of course.

FRANKLIN FINISHED WASHING THE DINNER DISHES. THEY'D had leftovers that night, some of the spaghetti that Julie had made for her pa and her uncle, along with some pot roast from earlier in the week. The only light in the kitchen that was on was the one over the stove, next to the sink, just enough for Franklin to see what he was doing.

For a moment, Franklin wished that Mama was there, so he could explain himself to her. He knew she'd do nothing but glare at him if she were a ghost, call him all kinds of fool if she were alive.

But Franklin couldn't see any other way to go about it.

"Gotta do my duty," Franklin said softly to the empty kitchen.

He found Julie already asleep on the couch, her hands clasped protectively over her belly. He didn't want to wake her up, but she'd get an awful kink in her neck if she stayed that way.

"Come on darling, off to bed," Franklin said as he lifted one hand up.

Julie smiled up at him and sleepily rose to her feet. "Only one more week," she said.

Franklin knew she was talking about work. She'd be finished with her job, taking two weeks off before the baby was due just to get everything else ready.

Before Julie could take a step, she grunted, slipping both her hands around her belly. Franklin watched, fascinated, as a ripple went across her skin.

Julie looked up at Franklin, the worry evident. "Damn it!" she said.

"What's up?" Franklin said, the worry giving him chills, like an army of ghosts just come tromping in.

Julie looked down. A wet patch spread across the inside of her thighs.

"I think my water just broke," she said. She gasped. "And that's another contraction."

Franklin froze. Normally, when things got bad, Franklin just got stubborn. Sometimes he got scared, but not often.

Not until a time like now. His heart didn't start racing but he could feel it pounding loud and hard. His hands grew clammy and sweat gathered in the small of his back.

"What should I do?" Franklin asked. "Do I call an ambulance?"

"Nope," Julie said with a grin followed by another quiet gasp. "But you get to drive me to the hospital."

Franklin gave a large gulp. He could do this. Just because he didn't like to drive a car didn't mean he couldn't. He'd even taken a spin in a zooped up race car that Julie's dad had been tweaking.

That didn't seem nearly as scary as driving Julie to the hospital.

Fortunately, even though the baby weren't due for a while, Julie already had a bag packed. Franklin grabbed that as Julie slowly made her way through the dining room, pausing every now and again for a breath.

"Seems we don't need to paint your toes pretty so the baby will come out," Franklin said, trying to make Julie smile.

"Seems not," she said as she eased herself into the passenger seat. Franklin had already put down one of those silver emergency blankets for Julie to sit on, so she wouldn't make a mess of the upholstery. Not that Franklin would have worried about that, but Julie had, and so had stashed the blanket in the console between the seats.

"You ready?" Franklin asked after he'd gotten both Julie and himself buckled in.

Out of the corner of his eye, he saw Sweet Bess standing guard in front of the house. It made him feel better, knowing that she was trying to protect the house while they was gone.

"No," Julie said with a laugh. "But I don't think what I want matters anymore."

"Matters to me," Franklin said. He reached over and gave Julie's hand a squeeze. "I love you. In case you was wondering."

Julie's smile could have lit up the entire neighborhood. "I love you, too. Now drive."

CHAPTER 10

FRANKLIN BREATHED A HUGE SIGH OF RELIEF WHEN HE turned the corner and saw the lights for the hospital up ahead. He'd done his darndest to make it here quickly. At least he knew the way and weren't about to get lost.

Still, merging with traffic, and waiting at lights, and getting his way across the county had worn every nerve he had left to bare thread. Julie had been on the phone with the hospital, letting them know they were coming. The operator had stayed on with Julie for a bit, talking her through the pain.

At least Franklin had gotten Julie to the hospital in under thirty minutes. He knew Julie could probably do it in twenty, maybe fifteen if she was really pushing her luck. But Franklin weren't about to risk any of their lives by doing something so foolish.

Attendants came out of the sliding doors with a wheelchair. They had Julie out of the car and were taking her inside in moments.

Franklin blinked, all his exhaustion slamming back hard

against his chest. He hadn't slept the night before, and now it looked like a second night without any rest.

Though more than one parent had already told him that he'd better get used to not sleeping.

Driving even more carefully, Franklin took the car out of the emergency spot and around to the side, into the parking lot. He locked the car, then had to go back and get Julie's bag. He was just locking the car a second time when the phone rang.

"Hi, Darryl," Franklin said as he walked quickly back toward the hospital. "What's up?"

"Tommy's missing," Darryl said. He sounded worried, more worried than the first time.

"Well, I'm at the hospital with Julie. She's gone into labor," Franklin told Darryl. "You sure Tommy's gone?"

"He left a note this time," Darryl said. "Said he's gone to do his duty. And he left a couple of those *Have You Seen Me* posters underneath it."

That stopped Franklin cold. "What does that mean?"

"I don't know. Why don't you tell me?" Darryl snapped. "You've always been talking on and on about how you have to do your duty to the ghosts. What the hell does Tommy think he's doing?"

"Who's he been reading fortunes for?" Franklin asked. He paused after he walked back into the hospital, blinking, trying to make his eyes adjust to the bright light after being in the dark.

"Don't know," Darryl said. "He won't tell us. But you know that room I made him? In the basement?"

"Yup," Franklin said, still waiting.

"Well, I think it was a bad idea to put him down there. The whole room's cold. It's like a freezer down there sometimes."

Ice trickled down Franklin's spine. He glanced over his shoulder, but there weren't no ghost.

"You remember that time Sweet Bess ran through you?" Franklin asked quietly, not moving from the door.

"Yes," Darryl said slowly.

"Is it like that?"

"Damn it, Franklin! Yes. It's exactly like that," Darryl said. "What kind of ghosts have been visiting my boy?"

"I think I know," Franklin said. "It's the young boys who been visiting me. They wanted Tommy to tell their fortunes for them. I think...I think he saw something in the cards. Something that he thought he could do for them."

"Then where's he gone?" Darryl asked.

"To the ice cream man's house."

It took Franklin a while to find where they'd stashed Julie. They'd taken her right up to a room, but it wasn't in the maternity ward. They had her one hall over, with the cardiac patients.

Franklin found Julie lying in bed, dressed in a white hospital gown. An IV was already attached to her arm, giving her fluids.

"How you doing?" Franklin asked, coming in and kissing her forehead.

"I'm all right," Julie said. She sounded sleepy. "I think this kid is gonna be as stubborn as you."

"Why's that?" Franklin said, holding Julie's hand. It seemed so small and fragile just then, though he knew that Julie was one of the strongest people in the world.

"'Cause just after I got here, all ready to give birth, the

contractions stopped." Julie frowned. "Or at least I think they did. The pain and pressure just…went away."

"Is that a bad sign? Or a good sign?" Franklin asked, trying not to be too worried until he knew he needed to be.

Julie shrugged. "Not really a sign of anything. Babies have their own way of doing things. Means I could go into labor again in the next five minutes. Or that I won't start getting contractions again for another forty-eight hours."

"Oh," Franklin said. He felt dizzy all of a sudden and wanted to sit down.

"What's going on?" Julie asked.

"Tommy's gone missing," Franklin admitted. "Dang it! I didn't mean to tell you that. You pretend I didn't just say that." He was so tired now there just weren't any filters on his mouth.

"Darryl can't find him?"

Franklin shook his head. "I'm wondering if it's the cards that are hiding him, or the ghosts. Darryl's wondering if maybe the basement is haunted now." Franklin remembered how cold it had seemed over there. He'd been wondering himself if there were ghosts there that he just couldn't see.

Maybe boys playing hide and seek.

"So what are you doing here?" Julie asked.

"What do you mean?" Franklin said, feeling stupid.

"You need to go find Tommy," Julie said firmly. "Right now."

"Don't you need me here?" Franklin said, trying not to be hurt.

"Got the most important part of you right here," Julie said, patting her belly. "I'm in good hands. Doctor is on her way. There's not much for you to do right now but sit and wait. May as well go do something useful, keep your cousin out of jail."

Franklin snorted. "You know, that's the second time that

someone's said I'm supposed to be the sane, reasonable one of the pair of us. You know how crazy that sounds?"

Julie grinned. "I do. Now git."

"Yes, ma'am," Franklin said. He stood up. "You sure you're gonna be okay?"

"As long as you don't end up in jail," Julie said truthfully. "And even then, we'll be okay."

"I'll be back as soon as I can," Franklin told her, kissing her temple.

"You find that boy," Julie said, grabbing his hand and holding on to it tightly. "I want all the family together before this baby comes."

"Absolutely," Franklin promised. He kissed her again, then made himself walk out of the hospital room because he knew if he stayed even a moment longer, he'd never leave.

His family needed him. All of his family.

DARRYL PICKED FRANKLIN UP AT THE HOSPITAL. THERE weren't ever a lot of traffic in town, and now that it was after ten PM, there was even less. Orange clouds reflected the streetlights and hid the stars. Cold winds blew up the canyons formed by the buildings on either side.

Franklin didn't like how worried Darryl looked. He had lines down the sides of his face, like he was tensing his cheeks, holding in a howl.

"We'll find him," Franklin assured Darryl.

He weren't sure about the mean look Darryl threw at him. He took a deep breath, settling himself further into the seat.

Funny. Darryl being angry at him and Tommy missing

hadn't riled Franklin up anywhere near as much as Julie starting labor. Franklin felt almost calm, now.

"What is it?" Franklin asked. He knew they needed to clear the air before the wounds festered.

"You and your damned ghosts are gonna get my boy killed," Darryl spat out as he pulled into traffic.

"If you really think that, then why the hell have you come to fetch me?" Franklin said. He couldn't make this right. He had his ghosts. He couldn't deny them, or his duty.

Darryl were just gonna have to choose between being mad at Franklin for who he was, or forgiving him and moving on.

"'Cause you're also the best chance I have for getting him back," Darryl admitted. "You and your damned ghosts."

"What are you talking about?" Franklin said. He'd thought for sure that they'd be trying to track the path of the ice cream truck, starting up on Ellis Street.

"The ghosts that Tommy told the fortunes for. They started in your backyard, right?" Darryl asked.

"You can't track a ghost," Franklin told Darryl. "It ain't like they're moving across the ground or something. One minute they're there, the next, they're gone."

"I know that," Darryl said, impatience making his voice higher than usual. "But you can track your ghosts, right?"

Franklin shook his head. "I can't call 'em to me, like a cat or a dog."

Darryl glared at Franklin. "Fine. But sometimes they just appear, right? Which is why you don't normally drive a car?"

"Yes," Franklin said. "Can never predict that."

"Then we're gonna drive around until either one of them pops out at you, or they stop hiding where Tommy's at," Darryl said.

"All right," Franklin said. He didn't see much point. He'd rather be waiting in the hospital with Julie.

Except that he knew that Darryl had to be doing something. Just sitting around and idle would kill Darryl. Hell, Georgia probably suggested that Darryl go looking, just because he'd be driving her crazy as well.

Now, Franklin knew that sometimes he had *feelings* about things. Like that one old house across town that seemed filled with unhappy ghosts though he'd never actually seen a ghost on the property. He sometimes rode his bike home the long way, just because it felt right. Generally, nothing happened on those longer trips, but sometimes he would see something that he wouldn't have, like the time he spotted that fresh patch of wild blackberries that he and Karl came back to harvest and sell.

The first mistake Franklin made was closing his eyes. He'd not had any sleep and he blinked them back open fast enough, before he'd actually fallen asleep.

That wouldn't work.

He didn't know what Eddie had meant by *expanding your senses into the universe*. That seemed awfully stupid to him. Franklin liked his senses just where they was, thank you very much.

"I'm gonna try to find some ghosts," Franklin announced to Darryl. "Turn down here," he directed.

Darryl had headed out of town where the hospital had been located, along the backroads to Katherinesville. Darryl obliged and turned onto the two-lane street. They quickly drove out of neighborhoods and into fields. Dark shapes slumbered near the fences, probably cattle. Farm houses loomed across large expanses of land. The few streetlights were just pools of brightness stringing the darkness together.

Franklin took a deep breath. He rolled down the window just an inch so he could breathe the fresh air.

"You're worse than any dog, sticking his nose out the window," Darryl complained as he turned the heat up another notch.

Franklin just shook his head and didn't pay him no heed. That was just Darryl.

"Tell me what happens when you try to track Tommy," Franklin said after a moment. He didn't know what was hiding the boy from his pa. Were it the ghosts? The cards? A combination of each?

Darryl shook his head. "I don't. That's the problem. It's a big nothing."

"What happens when you think about Pete or Joanne? Or even Georgia?" Franklin asked.

Darryl's tight grip on the steering wheel loosened. As the cabin of the truck was so dim, it was the only way that Franklin could see that Darryl had relaxed a little.

"They're warm," Darryl announced after a moment. "I got a strong sense of where they are. If I was a bird, I could fly direct to them, no stops. With the truck, I may end up making some wrong turns, but I'd get there."

"And now think about Tommy again," Franklin coached.

Darryl nodded. Even in the dim light Franklin could see Darryl's jaw tighten.

"There's nothing. Just a Tommy sized hole," Darryl said.

"Can you find that hole, then?" Franklin asked.

Darryl opened his mouth, then closed it again. "Maybe. Maybe not. You have any luck tracking your ghosts?"

Franklin closed his eyes for a brief moment. He felt a little dizzy, but he pushed that to the side. "I just get the feeling we're going in the right direction," he said after a bit.

Maybe it were just his imagination. Maybe he was a bit too much like Darryl, and it felt better because he was doing *something* and not just sitting around waiting.

"Turn here," Franklin told Darryl suddenly.

Darryl was already making the right turn.

"How'd you know what direction to go in?" Franklin asked. It had been a cross street, running both ways.

Darryl shrugged. "Just knew. It's one of the direct streets from Katherinesville."

The farms out here were divided by patches of wilderness, tall trees and blackberry brambles. Ditches ran along either side of the road, starting to fill with water from the fall rains after the hot summer. A row of tall silos standing guard like big bullets ran along the right side, then more trees.

"Is Tommy on his bike?" Franklin asked after a bit.

"Yup," Darryl said.

"Can you track the bike?" Franklin said after a bit.

"Don't know," Darryl said. "Hadn't tried it."

He pulled over to the side of the road. There weren't much there, just a strip of concrete wide enough for a set of tires on the other side of the yellow line. Darryl put on his hazard lights, letting other cars know that he was there.

Darryl took a deep breath. Franklin didn't say anything, though he wanted to tease Darryl about needing the air in the cab as much as he did. Darryl pressed himself back in his seat, stretching his arms out and closing his eyes.

Finally, Darryl sat back up, nodding. "It's hard to trace. Particularly since Tommy's taking all roads. But I think I got scent of him now."

"Good," Franklin said as Darryl turned off his hazards and started driving again. "You ain't as useless as you look, Cuz."

"Neither are you."

They had a few wrong turns after that before Franklin was hit by a cold patch so hard he nearly fell off his seat. "Stop!"

Darryl looked over at Franklin who'd started shivering. They was outside of one of those huge subdivisions that had at one point been someone's farm. They'd gotten trapped in there for a bit, unable to find their way out of all the damned cul-de-sacs. All the houses they'd passed by were dark by now. The clouds had cleared off and brilliant stars peaked through the night sky.

"We passed through a real cold patch back there," Franklin explained. "Probably a bunch of ghosts."

Darryl threw the truck into reverse.

Franklin shivered harder as they passed through the spot again. Even his lungs felt cold, making it hard to breathe. The cold spot was located on the far side of a long driveway leading up to a house.

"Park here," Franklin informed Darryl. "We'll go by foot, now."

Darryl threw a questioning look at Franklin, then shrugged. "You're the boss," he said. He parked the truck off the road and climbed out, then reached behind his seat and pulled out a backpack.

Franklin knew it contained a lot of gear, like emergency blankets, extra flashlights and batteries, power bars, water bottles, and so on. He wouldn't be surprised if this one had an extra med kit or two tucked away, and maybe gear like splints.

Then Darryl pulled out his riffle.

"No," Franklin said, putting his hand on Darryl's arm. "I can't let you take that with you."

"You don't have a choice," Darryl said, talking as though through gritted teeth.

"Yes, I do have a choice," Franklin said. "I can drop you here and now."

Darryl snorted.

Franklin continued. "You ain't gonna put yourself at danger. I won't let you."

"I wouldn't be the one in danger," Darryl said, hefting the gun.

"That's not what I meant. You'd be putting yourself in danger of getting arrested," Franklin told him, working to keep his voice gentle. "I am not gonna be responsible for getting your ass thrown into jail. Or shot by the police not believing that you ain't gonna shoot them. Put it back. Now."

"You ain't tough enough to stop me," Darryl said, though he sounded just a touch wary.

"Don't need to be tough," Franklin said. "Just more stubborn than you."

"But..." Darryl stared at Franklin.

Franklin didn't want to beat his cousin up. That weren't his way. However, if Darryl was gonna be stupid about it, Franklin wouldn't have a choice but to try to knock some sense into Darryl's thick head.

The darkness hid what was going through Darryl's head; however, Franklin could tell the moment that he finally reached the conclusion that Franklin was dead serious.

"I'm gonna blame you if it turns out we needed that riffle," Darryl said after he slid it back into the truck.

"I will, too," Franklin assured Darryl. He couldn't say for certain if he was making the right decision. It felt right, though.

They weren't dealing with a creature, not as far as Franklin had been able to figure out. Not a summoned demon or a cursed knife.

Just a man who shoulda known better than to prey on kids.

There weren't no sneaking up this driveway. A few trees lined the edges of the neatly trimmed yard, not enough to provide cover. The windows of the house in front of them had a clear view of the road.

As there weren't any lights on in the house, Franklin felt more confident walking up the road. Darryl kept looking around, as if expecting something or someone to rise suddenly out of the grass and attack them. But he weren't truly hunting, that much Franklin could tell. Darryl moved at ordinary speed, no gift lending him its grace.

They'd gotten about a quarter of the way down the driveway when Franklin saw a dark spot just off the side of the road. "What's that?" he asked, a chill running down his spine when he saw it.

Darryl shone his flashlight on the spot. "Tommy's bike," he said grimly. "Come on."

Now Darryl ran with the speed of a worried parent. Franklin ran with him, his own worry edging him on.

They'd just about reached the circular part of the driveway in front of the house when Darryl suddenly took off in a burst of speed that Franklin couldn't hope to match.

He saw the dark figure just a moment later.

Tommy, stubbornly walking up toward the door.

"What do you think you're doing?" Darryl asked, grabbing Tommy by the arm and shaking him.

Tommy shook his head, looking dazed. Instead of answering his pa, he stood up straighter. He glared down at the hand Darryl had wrapped around his arm, then back up at Darryl.

Franklin was glad that Darryl seemed to be listening to sense, because he let go of Tommy. But then he cross his arms over his chest and just glared at the boy. "What are you doing," Darryl said, his tone flat and mean.

"I'm gonna stop him," Tommy said with a glance over his shoulder at the darkened house.

"No, you ain't," Darryl said. He didn't reach out to grab Tommy again, but Franklin could tell he wanted to.

Before Tommy could start his arguing, Franklin stepped closer. "Darryl's right," Franklin said softly. "You ain't gonna stop him. I am."

Both of them turned to glare at Franklin.

Franklin felt himself widening his stance, ready to fight both of them at the same time. "You're gonna take your son home," Franklin told Darryl. Then he turned and talked to Tommy. "This ain't your fight. You got others that'll come to you. But this here's something that I gotta do."

"But the ghosts came to me," Tommy said stubbornly. "They was asking me to do something."

Franklin nodded. "They asked me, too," he said. "And I was listening to them. But they're boys. They didn't understand that these things take time."

"He grabbed another boy," Tommy said.

"Then I'll get him out, too," Franklin assured the young man. "Now, you go home with your pa. And you hug your ma and apologize to her for making her so worried. And you *tell* me or your pa or your ma before you go off and do something like this next time."

"There won't be a next time," Darryl said.

Franklin snorted. "Do you even see who you're talking to? The only reason he ain't as stubborn as you is because he's still growing into it."

"But—" Tommy started.

"You gotta trust us, son," Franklin said. "Please. We'll do the right thing."

Tommy still just looked stubborn.

"All right, so adults don't always have the best track record when it comes to not screwing things up," Franklin admitted. "But you know your Uncle Franklin. You know I'll make it right."

Tommy paused for a moment, considering. Finally, he nodded. A sigh went through him and the boy suddenly seemed a bit smaller than he'd been, like he'd been puffed up and had just let go of all the extra air filling him.

Cold passed through and around Franklin. He couldn't see the ghosts, but he knew they was there.

"I'll stop him," Franklin promised Darryl, Tommy, and the ghosts surrounding them.

He didn't know how, but he knew it was his duty, as much as helping ghosts pass.

CHAPTER 11

FRANKLIN DIDN'T FEEL RIGHT GOING AND KNOCKING ON Mr. Orville's door. It were late, near midnight now. But he didn't think this could wait until morning.

Before Darryl and Tommy had left, Darryl had shone his flashlight on a large shape looming on the left side of the house.

The ice cream truck sat there. Though Franklin didn't have any ghosts leading the way, he knew he was in the right place.

After a moment to collect his thoughts, Franklin finally rang the doorbell.

It surprised him that Mr. Orville answered almost immediately.

"Yes?" he asked, peering blearily at Franklin. His thick glasses was smudged, making his big blue eyes seem even more watery and out of focus. He still wore his gray ice cream uniform, with a fuzzy brown cardigan over that and brown slippers.

The front hallway opened up to a large long living room on the right, with a staircase on the left and closed doors behind it, leading to the rest of the house. A fireplace sat tucked away in the far corner of the living room, providing a warm cheery glow. The couch under the windows had blankets piled up on it.

It seemed like a perfectly normal house, if a bit shabby and run down. Franklin would bet there'd be cobwebs in the corners if he was looking in the light of day.

"Sorry, sir," Franklin said slowly. "We was just conducting a house-to-house search. Have you seen this boy?" he asked, bringing out the one *Have You Seen Me* flier of Hollis that Tommy had been carrying.

Mr. Orville looked shocked. "Why would you be asking me about that?" Then he blinked and got a sly look on his face. "I've seen you before, haven't I?" he said. "You got a boy at Mayville, right?"

That was one of the bigger high schools in the area.

"No, sir," Franklin said. "My first is due any time now." Julie hadn't called him yet, so Franklin knew she hadn't really gone back into labor.

"I remember the birth of my boy," Mr. Orville said. "It was one of the most special nights of my life."

"Tell me about it," Franklin said. "I can't wait for the birth of mine."

Mr. Orville smiled at him and nodded. "You got some sleepless nights ahead of you. But you must treasure each and every one of them."

"Because they grow up so fast?" Franklin asked. He kept waiting for a sign that something was wrong here, for the ghosts to show up.

Something. Anything.

"And they slip away before you ever really get to know them," Mr. Orville said. He shook his head.

Sorrow beat at Franklin. He suddenly had the impression of

a broken man, beat down by the world and barely hanging on. Losing his only son had damaged Mr. Orville in ways that Franklin didn't even want to imagine.

"Afraid I can't help you," Mr. Orville said, nodding toward the flier Franklin still had in his hand. "Good luck with your search, and good night."

A soft sigh came from the living room on the right. The blankets on the couch suddenly shifted. A boy sat up.

"Now, excuse me, I need to go tend to my boy," Mr. Orville said, trying to close the door on Franklin. "He's been sick, so I've been letting him sleep down here."

"That ain't your boy," Franklin said, taking a chance. He didn't think Mr. Orville would have adopted another. Wasn't sure he could.

A look of panic washed over Mr. Orville's face. Then the stubbornness took over. "Is too," Mr. Orville said.

"No, he ain't," Franklin said. "You got some other boy you're trying to make yours." It was the only thing that made sense to Franklin, why Mr. Orville would be taking the boys he'd been snatching.

"He's mine," Mr. Orville said, his voice rising. "You can't take him from me."

"He ain't yours," Franklin said. He shoved the door open wider.

Mr. Orville fell back into the room. "No!" he wailed, his heart breaking all over again. "I'll make him mine. And I'll make him mind, too. He's the right one."

"How could you take the lives of the other boys?" Franklin asked, perplexed. "When you know what it is that their parents will be going through?"

"They didn't deserve to keep them," Mr. Orville said

snappishly. "You don't know how those boys been treated. I see it every day at the bus stop."

"The parents did the best they could," Franklin said stubbornly. He knew that parents didn't always do right by their kids. It were a challenge he was gonna try to live up to. "You had your chance. Now let this boy go."

The boy in question had laid his head back on the couch. Was he actually sick? Or had Mr. Orville already done something to him?

"No," Mr. Orville said. "And you can't make me." He sneered. "Who are the cops going to believe when I call them?"

"You can't keep him," Franklin said. He knew that he wouldn't have a chance in hell if Mr. Orville decided to press charges against him. Sheriff Thompson might believe him but would a judge?

And Franklin had the terrible feeling that when the police arrived there wouldn't be a new boy for them to find. Not anymore.

"You can't keep doing this," Franklin said. He took a step toward Mr. Orville. "You've got to let these boys grow up in their own families."

"This will be the last one," Mr. Orville said, throwing a glance at the figure who'd laid back down on the couch. He took a step backwards, into the living room.

"No, it won't," Franklin said. "There'll be something wrong with him. Like there were with the others. Then the next. And the next. He's not your son. He never will be."

"Who's going to stop me?" Mr. Orville said as he picked up his cell phone from where it'd been sitting on a side table.

"Me," Franklin said.

He didn't want to lay hands on the man. It weren't his style.

But he knew he had to do something. He grabbed Mr. Orville's hand, the one holding the cell phone.

The ghosts in the room was waiting for something, some sort of sign. Even though Franklin couldn't see them, couldn't feel the cold they always brought with them, he knew they was there. Waiting. Little boys hiding. Scared.

"I'm not gonna let you do this again," Franklin said stubbornly hanging on while Mr. Orville tried to twist out of his grasp. "It stops here."

Suddenly, ghosts sprang up around them. Franklin counted at least six boys. Were there others who'd already passed on? He was afraid to ask.

Franklin recognized Andrew and Hollis standing right behind Mr. Orville.

Before Mr. Orville could do something foolish like try to throw a punch at Franklin, Andrew pushed his way *through* the man's body.

A cold shock ran up Franklin's arm, from where he was holding onto Mr. Orville's wrist.

Mr. Orville gasped at the feeling.

"That's one of the boys you killed," Franklin told him.

"No," Mr. Orville said. "I didn't kill them. They took their own lives. They wouldn't obey me. Wouldn't accept me as their father. They made me do it, don't you see?"

Franklin swallowed down his angry words. He was plenty mad, but it weren't his place to be yelling at the man.

No, it was the ghosts who needed to be speaking now.

Hollis pushed his way through Mr. Orville next. Then the next ghost, and the next. Sometimes they brushed against Franklin as well, making all the goosebumps raise up on his skin and giving him the shivers something fierce.

All Franklin had to do was to hold on. To say *no*. To not let Mr. Orville run away from his past.

This time, it was up to the ghosts to do their duty. To stop this man.

The boys ran at Mr. Orville now, almost like a game, circling him and pushing their way through the old man's body. His eyes grew cloudy and glazed, like an icy film was covering them. His face turned blue and he gasped for breath.

Franklin stubbornly held on, even as his own teeth started chattering. He wished for one of Darryl's emergency blankets, anything to hold in what little heat he had.

For a moment, Mr. Orville's eyes cleared. He glanced at Franklin and nodded. It were like he was suddenly seeing clearly, seeing what he'd been doing to the boys and their families, not just thinking about himself.

Franklin took a step back, knowing that Mr. Orville had finally accepted his fate. He held his arms open, as if he were about to embrace the boys. They formed a line now, and passed through him one last time, pushing their anger and fear and the chill of the grave through Mr. Orville's body.

When Mr. Orville's knees gave out and he fell to the floor, Franklin knew the old man was dead. Coroner would probably declare it a heart attack.

The boys gathered around the body for a moment. They held hands and bowed their heads, like they was saying a prayer for the old man. Then they started growing fuzzy, changing into mist and fog instead of ghosts.

After a few moments, they'd all passed on. Franklin knew he wouldn't be seeing any of them ever again. They was at peace, finally.

The room still felt as cold as though an ice storm had blown through.

Franklin walked over to the couch to see to the boy there. He were about the same size as Hollis, skinny and young. Franklin picked him up, blankets and all, then carried him out of the house. The boy's breath smelled of nasty chemicals. Had he been drugged?

After putting the boy on the ground as gently as he could, Franklin called 911.

Then sat and waited for the sheriff to come.

"You thought you saw a boy playing around here?" Sheriff Thompson said.

"Yes, sir," Franklin said. He finally had his own blanket wrapped around him, though he sometimes still shivered with cold. The EMTs who'd come in the ambulance had assumed Franklin was in shock. They wouldn't know that it were just the ghosts. Franklin would feel warm again, in a day or so.

"So you decided to come and confront Mr. Orville?" the sheriff asked. His beady eyes stared hard at Franklin, angry as two living hornets.

"I did," Franklin admitted. He told the sheriff his story again. "I showed him the flier of Hollis. And he had a heart attack and died when he looked at it."

"What really happened?" Sheriff Thompson pressed.

Franklin sighed. "You gonna press charges against me?" he asked. He was so tired now. And he still had to get back to the hospital and wait for the baby.

Sheriff shrugged. "Not sure what I'd charge you with," he admitted. "You weren't breaking and entering. You did find the missing boy, still alive. And they're gonna start digging in the backyard come morning."

Both Franklin and Sheriff Thompson shivered in unison. There were mounds of fresh dirt in the backyard. They both knew what was buried there.

"Then why do you want to know?" Franklin asked. "I stopped him."

Damn it! He was too tired. He shouldn't have said that.

"How?" Sheriff Thompson asked. He sighed. "I just need to know that I don't have another killer on my hands."

Franklin shook his head. "I didn't kill him. The ghosts did."

"The what?" Sheriff Thompson said. He sounded more tired than angry.

"You wouldn't believe me if I told you," Franklin said.

Sheriff Thompson peered more closely at Franklin. "I know that people say you talk with ghosts. So why don't I tell you what I think happened?"

"Sounds good to me," Franklin said. What did it look like outside, to a stranger?

"I think the ghosts told you to come here," the sheriff said. He shook his head. "Lord, I can't believe I'm saying this. I think they got you here, and that you helped them kill this man."

"And what if that were the truth, Sheriff?" Franklin asked. "What are you gonna do about it?"

"I don't want no vigilantes running around my town," the sheriff said. "People need to follow the law, not take it into their own damned hands." He sighed. "I wish you would have told me."

Franklin shrugged. "You don't believe in ghosts anyway."

"Yeah, but I believe you," Sheriff Thompson said.

"You arrested me," Franklin pointed out. He was finally starting to get a bit warmer. Or maybe he were just mad.

"Kind of had to, on account of a favor with the sheriff from the next county," Sheriff Thompson admitted.

He paused and looked over at the house. Yellow police tape covered the front door, and a police officer sat in his car a ways off, making sure that no once came any closer. Not until the Crime Unit from Louisville would show up, sometime in the morning.

"Is this gonna happen again?" Sheriff Thompson finally asked.

"I don't know," Franklin said. "Are there more killers in the neighborhood with bodies buried in the backyard?"

"Lord, I hope not," Sheriff Thompson said. Then he shrugged. "Probably not. This isn't Seattle."

Franklin didn't know what exactly Seattle had to do with anything, though he supposed maybe they had a lot of strange people up there.

"This doesn't happen again, I won't need to do anything, will I?" Franklin asked.

The sheriff nodded. Then he pulled out his wallet and handed Franklin a business card. "You keep this," he said. The front had the sheriff's name, telephone number, and email. There was writing on the back that Franklin couldn't make out in the dark.

"What's it say?" Franklin asked.

"Now, you only use this when you absolutely need it," the sheriff said. "Think of it as a get out of jail free card."

Franklin nodded and carefully tucked the card away in his own wallet. "Thank you."

"Don't let this happen again," Sheriff Thompson warned, waving at the house, indicating everything that had gone on.

"Can't promise that," Franklin said.

Someone needed to be there to say no when Franklin started seeing too many ghosts, ghosts who hadn't died of natural causes.

"I know," the sheriff said. "Now, get out of here. The deputy waiting on the road will take you back to the hospital."

"Thank you, Sheriff," Franklin said.

He weren't planning on this ever happening again.

Only if he absolutely had to.

FRANKLIN COULDN'T BELIEVE HOW TINY BABY CHELSEY was. And how perfect. She had ten perfect little fingers. Ten perfect little toes tucked away in booties. Her skin was a perfect mixture of white and brown, making her look like she'd been dipped in milk chocolate. Fuzzy black hair covered her head, and her eyes was a dark brown.

Julie lay with her eyes closed on the hospital bed. She'd gone into labor just as Franklin had arrived at the hospital. Hadn't even taken two hours, and the baby had come easy.

Darryl and the others would be coming by in the morning, welcome Chelsey into the family. She'd have cousins to play with and look up to. Aunts and Uncles to tell her stories and make her laugh.

And a proud pa who would protect his little girl against all the monsters.

Didn't matter what happened next. If it were a creature or a man.

As long as Franklin was there to just say no, everything was gonna be all right.

ABOUT THE AUTHOR

Leah Cutter writes page-turning fiction in exotic locations, such as a magical New Orleans, the ancient Orient, Hungary, the Oregon coast, rural Kentucky, Seattle, Minneapolis, and many others.

She writes literary, fantasy, mystery, science fiction, and horror fiction. Her short fiction has been published in magazines like *Alfred Hitchcock's Mystery Magazine* and *Talebones*, anthologies like Fiction River, and on the web. Her long fiction has been published both by New York publishers as well as small presses.

Find Leah's books here.

Follow her blog at www.LeahCutter.com.

Reviews

It's true. Reviews help me sell more books. If you've enjoyed this story, please consider leaving a review of it on your favorite site.

Come someplace new...

Are you a traveler? Do you enjoy exploring strange new worlds, new cultures, new people?

Sign up for my newsletter and I'll start you on your travels with a free copy of my book, *The Island Sampler*.

I will never spam you or use your email for nefarious purposes. You can also unsubscribe at any time.

http://www.LeahCutter.com/newsletter/

ABOUT KNOTTED ROAD PRESS

Knotted Road Press fiction specializes in dynamic writing set in mysterious, exotic locations.

Knotted Road Press non-fiction publishes autobiographies, business books, cookbooks, and how-to books with unique voices.

Knotted Road Press creates DRM-free ebooks as well as high-quality print books for readers around the world.

With authors in a variety of genres including literary, poetry, mystery, fantasy, and science fiction, Knotted Road Press has something for everyone.

Knotted Road Press
www.KnottedRoadPress.com